THE KAISER'S LAST KISS

Also by Alan Judd

A Breed of Heroes
Short of Glory
The Noonday Devil
Tango
The Devil's Own Work
Legacy

NON-FICTION
Ford Madox Ford
The Quest for C
First World War Poets
(with David Crane)
The Office Life Little Instruction Book
(as Holly Budd)

ALAN JUDD

The Kaiser's Last Kiss

HarperCollins*Publishers*

HarperCollins*Publishers*
77–85 Fulham Palace Road,
Hammersmith, London W6 8JB

www.fireandwater.com

Published by HarperCollins*Publishers* 2003
1 3 5 7 9 8 6 4 2

A catalogue record for this book
is available from the British Library

ISBN 0 0 00 712446 5

Typeset in Meridien by Palimpsest Book Production Limited,
Polmont, Stirlingshire

Printed and bound in Great Britain
by Clays Ltd, St Ives plc

This novel is a work of fiction.
Although some of the characters portrayed in it
are based on historical figures, the events are a work
of the author's imagination.

To Katie

ONE

The Kaiser was chopping logs. In the summer air his strokes echoed through the trees, across the park and gardens and into Huis Doorn itself, where those of the household would be listening. So long as they could hear him, they would know that all was well with their Kaiser that morning. They could relax, he thought, and be happy, or busy about their work, which was to his mind the same thing.

His strokes were regular but the pauses were longer now. At eighty, it was an achievement to split a log at all – to see it, even – let alone do it daily. Nearly every day since his exile in 1918 he had chopped or sawn. At first he had imagined the logs his enemies, the poltroons who had betrayed him and urged him to flee so that they could grab power for themselves. Gradually, he had ceased to care about that bunch of pigs but had continued felling because it made him feel better, restoring his sense of achievement. Twenty thousand trees felled in the first eleven years of exile; that was something. Since then another twelve years during which he had not kept such meticulous records; not quite another twenty thousand, perhaps, but still a good number. His best was 2,590 in one week – Christmas week – after he had moved here to Doorn after Amerongen, the other Dutch place. What would the Englishman, Gladstone, another elderly tree-feller, have said to that? It might have silenced him, and his tribe. Tree-feller, tree-fella, it punned in English. He would entertain people with it.

Bismarck would have had something to say to it, of course. He was a tree-lover who used to try to plant a tree for every one that Gladstone felled and then write to him about it, to boast. Well now, he, Wilhelm II, had bested them both, because he had felled more and planted more than either.

Bismarck had something to say to everything, that was his trouble. That was why it was right to get rid of him all those years ago, to drop the pilot, as someone put it. It was right then, anyway. Perhaps he might not have made the same decision now. But that was then, when everything was different. When you are young you do not understand how different then and now are because you have lived only in now and it feels as if that is where you will always live. You do not realise that your now – and you – are becoming then. And when you realise how completely now has become then, how different it is, it is like the fall of the axe. It splits you off from all these younger people who, however much they think they know or understand, cannot feel life as it was then. The pulse of it, that was the thing, always, with everything, and that is what cannot be conveyed.

The Kaiser swung the axe again but this time it bounced violently, jarring his arm as if the log – oak, it looked like – were stone. It was a knotted old log, cross-grained, compacted, irreducible. He blamed Bismarck because he had been thinking of him. Even from his grave that cross-grained old man with the soul of a Pomeranian tenant-farmer still had the power to interpose himself wherever you looked, to make everything awkward, to turn things into problems which only he could solve. They were barely more than peasants, those Bismarcks, all of them. Their servants pulled wine corks with the bottles between their knees in front of you and there were always dogs around the table. The old man fed the dogs from his dinner plate, holding it while they licked it. Perhaps it was the very plate that he himself, the Kaiser, might have eaten from next time. That was a metaphor: Bismarck really cared more for his dog than for his Kaiser.

The Kaiser lowered his axe to the ground and, using the shaft as a prop, carefully lifted one foot. With the hard toe of his boot he nudged the knotted log off the chopping block, a massive section of beech trunk. Then he let go of the axe and stooped to pick up another log. It was hard with one hand because the log was too wide to grip and he had to roll it up the side of the beech trunk. When he was younger he might have exercised his left arm by trying to ease the log into a central position on the block, but he didn't bother much with that arm now. A withered, blighted thing, from birth three inches shorter than its mate, he could hold with it but not lift or push much. God and he alone knew the youthful effort it cost him to learn to ride and to shoot, to learn above all not to be handicapped by this handicap. God had given it to him to make him tough, he had long ago decided. Years of solitary practice, holding oars out straight, had made his good right arm stronger than most men's two arms, with a grip that had been compared to that of John Sullivan, the boxing champion. But even John Sullivan was then. Who spoke of him now?

The axe split the new log clean, with a crack that echoed through the trees around the woodshed. Most men could not swing an axe with two arms as he still swung with one. There were plenty of trees ready for felling, more than he had days.

'Your Highness! Your Royal Highness!'

The Kaiser leant on his axe, turning slowly. The new Dutch maid was running through the rough grass bordering the park and the trees, clutching her white apron in one hand and waving with the other. When she called again he realised he had heard her before swinging at that last log but had not registered it. That happened, nowadays. He waited. He had heard and uttered many urgent summonses in life but now, robbed of their temporary urgency, it was clear that the things that would happen, happened, whether or not you buzzed about like a demented bluebottle. These days, he felt, there was nothing left to be urgent about. What would come would come soon enough, in its own time, and until then one chopped wood and shrugged one's shoulders at the world. He would not be hurried.

'– Highness!'

She almost stumbled in the last few yards. She was called Akki, his wife had told him. Breathlessness made her prettier than ever. A wisp of dark hair had come adrift from her bun and her smooth cheeks were coloured. Such beautiful skin, almost olive; he always wanted to touch it. Her grey eyes were quiet and thoughtful, cold as a March wind. Yet it was her hands above all that he looked for, slender, white, quick, full of energy but composed and controlled. With him it had always been the hands. First his mother's, then those of her friends and then – well, as many as he could get, in his youth. Beloved Dona, his first wife, she had good hands, but she knew what hands meant to him and throughout their marriage had ensured that all female servants had hands either like chicken claws or overgrown potatoes. She would never have permitted Akki to join the household. But Hermo, his new wife, did not know about this thing of his.

'– Highness!' The girl stood panting before him, her

4

grey eyes widened, one hand still clutching her apron. 'Highness, they have come. The Germans. They are here. Princess Hermine begs you to receive them. They are at the gate lodge.'

The Kaiser nodded. So the German Army was reunited with its Kaiser. The sky was not rent asunder, no fiery angels appeared, the voice of God remained silent. No longer the Kaiser's army, of course, but that fellow Hitler's, a corporal's army now. They would more likely view him as their prisoner than their king, unless – but it was useless to speculate. It had come to something when it was hard to take any interest in one's future. He was more interested in this girl's accent. She came from Friesland, Hermo had said, so Fries was presumably her first language, Dutch her second, German evidently her third. There was something odd about her German, not an accent – she had none – but more her speech rhythm, her way of saying things. It reminded him of his grandmother, Queen Victoria, whose German was similarly fluent and unaccented but with something of the same difference. Not that pretty little Akki, with her hypnotic hands, was in any way like Grandmama.

'Where are you from?' he asked. Her surprise was gratifying. It was always good to surprise them a little.

'From Leeuwarden, your Highness.' She went on, evidently thinking he had not understood her. 'The Princess begs you to come to the house because German soldiers have arrived. They have invaded Holland, as your Highness knows, and now they have come to see you. There is an officer with them. They are talking to our soldiers – your Dutch guard – at the gate lodge. The officer is from Schutzstaffel – SS.'

She used the term familiarly. Perhaps, like him, the Dutch people had studied Corporal Hitler's armed forces.

But he was Kaiser still, even if unrecognised in his own

5

land. The Kaiser did not dance attendance upon people; they came to him, whether they called themselves SS or Wehrmacht or the Pink Lederhosen. 'Tell the Empress I shall join her when I have finished here,' he said. 'And beg her to invite the Dutch guard commander, Major van Houten, for lunch.' He bent slowly and scooped up another log with his right hand. The girl bobbed a curtsey, backed a few steps, then turned and walked composedly through the rough grass towards the house. The morning dew lingered in the shade of the trees and she again clutched her apron. A pretty thing, he thought. Without doubt, were he a young man again, he would have sought to know her better, servant or no servant.

This log, too, he split with gratifying ease, plumb down the middle. It fell open like the book of life before God, a perfect symmetry. He would sign the two halves and give them to visitors or deserving Dutch locals. They seemed to appreciate signed logs as much as his books. Perhaps the logs stood for books he had never written.

He looked up at the barking of a dog. Arno, Hermo's bad-tempered German Shepherd, was bounding across the lawn towards the Dutch girl as if she were a stranger. She stopped and faced the dog. Her admonitions were firm, but taut and nervous. The dog had taken against her from the day of her arrival, and she obviously feared him. Mind you, Arno disliked most people, and sometimes he bit them. That could be quite funny. A green woodpecker laughed raucously in the trees. The Kaiser resumed his chopping.

After four more logs he lay down his axe. He had stayed long enough to show that he was in no hurry but not so long as seriously to upset Hermo, who would be excited and nervous. He strolled back along the track through the trees, contemplating his fine brick house as it came into view. It was a modest establishment compared with all his others, of course, but it was regularly and properly built, handsome in its own way. They had made many improvements so that it was now quite comfortable, even for the servants, and he had opened part of the park to the people of Doorn. From the day he arrived they had treated him with proper respect. Perhaps they had heard of his generosity to the people of Amerongen, the castle and village a few kilometres away where he had stayed when first in exile. He had built them a hospital, and signed many logs. With the Wehrmacht occupying Holland, however, it was possible that the people would turn against him, though perhaps not now that he was under the protection – presumably – of Herr Hitler. He had never met the fellow and had no idea what he planned but, for himself, he would die at Huis Doorn. Either way, they would have to carry him out.

Neither Arno nor the girl was any longer to be seen as he approached the house but his own three dachshunds were yapping on the terrace. The gate lodge was some distance away but the sounds of army lorries and shouted orders carried across the park, exciting the dogs. His long-range vision was still good and he glimpsed the field grey of the Wehrmacht as soldiers milled around the lodge. It was an arrow in his eye, a stab of familiarity, love, resentment and bitterness. Even the sound of boots on gravel was wrenchingly familiar. He turned his head and slowly mounted the steps. He was hot in his blue serge suit, Loden cape and hunting hat with feather, but did not wish to show it by removing anything. It was important that he should appear imperturbable, unhurried, his mind upon purposes invisible to others, higher purposes that rendered all else trivial. That was how emperors should appear.

In the cool of the house he removed cape and hat and, with more effort, his heavy leather boots, then changed into a lighter grey suit which he wore with gold tie-pin and the miniature *pour le mérite* in the buttonhole. Next, instead

7

of going to Princess Hermine, he went to his study and sat for a while at his high desk with the saddle seat. It was always comforting to see his own things around him and to look upon the portrait of dear Dona. Normally he had just a sandwich and a glass of port after sawing or chopping but now that he had invited Major van Houten they would be hurrying to prepare something more elaborate, although still essentially simple. That was how he liked his food. Unless, that was, the Wehrmacht had already arrested or dismissed the Dutchman, though an invitation from the Kaiser should give them pause. It would be an early sign of their attitude towards him.

When eventually he proceeded to the small dining-room he found lunch already laid, an informal affair of cold meats and cheeses with cherries, apples, strawberries, peaches and oranges. Hermo was waiting, wearing a voluminous light green dress that covered her like a bell tent and filled out when she moved so that her progress through the house reminded him of those East Indiamen you used to see in the English Channel during the days of sail. It suited her; she was a stately, sometimes a superbly stately, woman. There were difficulties, of course, things she did not always understand, but it was far better to have a new empress than none. She was a handsome woman, and young, relatively speaking. Many people, he thought, must surely be jealous.

'His name is SS Untersturmführer Krebbs,' she said, with the Kaiser not yet through the door. 'And his first name is Martin.'

The Kaiser stared expressionlessly, as always when affronted by the unexpected.

'The officer in charge of the soldiers, the one from Schutzstaffel,' she explained impatiently. Nervousness, or anxiety, had coloured her plump cheeks.

'So?' The Kaiser spoke quietly. It often intimidated

people. 'What have I to do with an SS Untersturmführer? That is the same as a Wehrmacht leutnant. A lieutenant, in other words. I have been a commissioned officer for seventy years. I was commissioned on my tenth birthday. Probably I was a leutnant before this puppy's grandfather was born.' He took a glass of his favourite sparkling red wine from the tray proffered by a servant. It was Assmushausen, a good German wine that he cut with water. 'Why should I wish to know his name, especially his first name? What is it to me? You are surely not suggesting I should run to see him?'

The Princess smiled. 'Of course not, my dear, that would be unthinkable. Forgive me if I gave that impression. The shock of seeing our German soldiers here, of seeing our own dear uniforms again, has unsettled me. I lack your experience.'

The Kaiser pinched her cheek. 'That is natural, my pet. You must not worry yourself. All in good time. Now, where is Major van Houten? It is unlike him to be unpunctual, especially for the Kaiser.'

'He is on his way, he is coming. He has to negotiate something with Untersturmführer Krebbs.' Princess Hermine slipped her hand through her husband's docile left arm, steering him carefully towards the window. He had aged several years in the past one. 'Such a beautiful day. Perhaps it is a good omen, perhaps Herr Hitler is right to occupy Holland.'

'It is necessary if he is to defeat Juda-England. We should have done so last time.'

'Of course. The High Command was criminally stupid not to let you run the war as you wished. But now our soldiers are here we must use their presence for maximum benefit for ourselves. Herr Hitler has done surprisingly well so far and as you know I think the Nazis have much to be said for them, but I am sure he will find he cannot manage it alone. He will need a respected figure who can unite the country, particularly the army, behind him. He can achieve nothing without the army, no matter what the strength of the Nazi party, and the army will not be content to be ruled by a corporal. It is bound to need its Kaiser again and they will have to invite you back. That is why it is important to show now that you do not spurn the Fatherland, no matter what errors were made in the past. The first report that Berlin receives of your reactions will be from Untersturmführer Krebbs, humble as he is. That is why, my dear, I think we should have invited him for lunch with us, not the Dutchman. The Dutch count for nothing now.'

The Kaiser moistened his lips with his wine, put down his glass and patted her hand. 'My dear, I have been working for that day since 1918 but I have less confidence than you that it will come. If Herr Hitler wished to know the Kaiser's views, he would surely not have sent so junior an officer. Your Untersturmführer is a mere guard commander, SS or no SS. Though he could be worse than that; he could be our gaoler. But you are right; we should not disregard what he represents. I shall receive him, in good time. Meanwhile, I wish to say farewell to our Dutchman. He has done his job with propriety and has even been a good companion, according to his lights, as the English say.'

Droplets of wine clung to the Kaiser's moustache, sparkling like tiny diamonds in the sunlight that came through the window. Though still substantial, the moustache was trimmed and turned conventionally down now, no longer the pointed, startled, upright growth known as 'Es ist erreicht!' The court barber, Haly, had made a fortune from the fashion that followed the Kaiser's adoption of his creation. He should have patented it himself, the Kaiser thought, and often said.

Towards the end of the drive, near the lodge, a Dutch Army lorry was now parked and some Dutch soldiers were loading equipment into it. The German soldiers were watching them. All appeared calm. They could make out the tall figure of Major van Houten talking to the young German officer, who was fondling the unusually quiescent Arno. Major van Houten broke off without saluting and strode up the drive towards the house. His long, lugubrious face and droll, unsmiling humour had often pleased the Kaiser. He would miss the gallant major. He patted the Princess's hand again.

'Invite your young man for dinner. Let us see how these people behave.'

'You are always right, dearest. You are so intelligent and wise.'

'But you must not invite him yourself. Send someone lowly.'

Lunch was a disappointment. The Kaiser had anticipated a pleasant and nostalgic farewell enlivened by the appreciative major's quiet irony. Instead, the major displayed neither amusement nor gratitude and allowed himself to appear visibly upset. Flushed with what the Kaiser had at first assumed merely to be heat and hurry, he claimed he had been detained by what he called the enemy. They were sending his soldiers back to the barracks which they now controlled, and had delayed sending him with them only because of the Kaiser's invitation.

That, at least, was gratifying to the Kaiser as an indication of respect, but he thought the use of the word 'enemy' gratuitous, if not offensive. However, he did not riposte as he might have but remarked only that he had not yet had an opportunity to address the new Wehrmacht guard.

'The officer is not Wehrmacht,' said Major van Houten. 'He is Schutzstaffel.'

The Kaiser's shrug was intended to suggest how little

such distinction mattered to him. 'And merely a leutnant, I understand, though these SS people call themselves something different. Where, I wonder, is his commanding officer?'

'In our barracks. He is in charge there.'

'I daresay I shall have to receive him one day. There is no hurry.' The Kaiser took his place at the table and began eating immediately. 'I trust that, as a military man, he will prove to have better manners than the Nazis.'

'Herr Hitler is said to be almost a perfect gentleman, and Herr Himmler is reportedly charming,' said the Princess, smiling at both men.

'My dear, one has to consider who it is that is making such judgements.' The Kaiser looked across at van Houten. It was then that he realised the man was weeping. He was eating and made no sound, but tears stood in his eyes. The Kaiser felt this was uncalled for, a gross over-indulgence, until it occurred to him that the major might have suffered a private grief. Something to do with his family, perhaps. He assumed the major had a family; he had never asked.

'Is everything all right, Major van Houten? Is all well with you?'

The major was still chewing, an action that made his face even sadder and funnier than usual. The Kaiser would tell Hermo about it later.

'Thank you, your Highness,' the major replied in his careful German. 'All is well with me. It is an emotional time, that is all. I apologise.' He inclined his head.

'My dear fellow, I understand. It is an emotional time for everyone, this new war. Where will it end? Wars are more easily started than stopped and my fear is that the machinery of warfare will run away with Herr Hitler, as it ran away with me. But he has done well so far, I grant him that. Tactically, he has done the correct things and has evidently learned the lessons of the High Command's failure last time.'

The major's spaniel eyes stared at the Kaiser's. 'Do you believe he has done the correct thing in invading us, your Highness?'

'Correct from his point of view, yes. Necessary. He has done the necessary thing. You see, major, this war is not with The Netherlands. It is important that you and your people understand that.' The Kaiser dabbed his lips with his napkin. 'No, this war is with France. It is the unfinished business that was prevented last time by England. Since then the French have behaved so badly in the territories they occupied after the armistice that a resumption of our war has become inevitable. They have been brutal to the German population, including children, and they wished to continue to starve them. They even tried to stop the English from lifting the blockade after the war. Did you know that more than three hundred and fifty thousand German people died as a result of the blockade – after the war, not during it? My own private secretary, von Islemann, lost four aunts because of it. Four aunts!'

The Kaiser stared across the table. There was something ridiculous in the notion of four aunts. How many aunts did a normal man need, for goodness' sake? Were they fat before the blockade? Four fat aunts fading away. It was a laughable thought, the sort of thing the major might normally remark upon, but he appeared to have lost his humour. The Kaiser felt he ought to demonstrate his own seriousness. 'People fear that because I have lived in Holland for over twenty years I do not know what the German people are thinking. But I do. I know very well what the German people think because people tell me and because I understand them here.' He thumped his chest with his right hand. 'It is not war itself they seek, but they hunger for justice and war is the only way. So for this new

13

war, they have, since 1918, been ready to march at once, to strangle the French. Well, now they are doing that but they cannot finish the job properly until they have driven Juda out of England, as they are driving them from the continent. The Jews and Anglo-American commercialism and materialism make it impossible for European peoples to live in decent peace and spiritual harmony. This war will be a divine judgement on Juda-England, you will see. That is why the soldiers of the Wehrmacht are here in Holland, Major van Houten. It is not against you or your country, and when the business is complete they will go. I promise you that.'

The Princess nodded. 'I do not believe the Nazis have anything against The Netherlands. Occupation is a regrettable necessity. It will pass, I am sure of that. It will become as water under the bridge.'

The major looked at her. 'No doubt it will pass, Princess. I too am sure of that. But not before much blood has sweetened the water beneath our bridges.'

The major's words hung in the air and rather soured luncheon, the Kaiser felt. The Dutchman was making more of the business than circumstances warranted. After all, it was not as if the Wehrmacht had done anything seriously unpleasant.

The Kaiser took his coffee standing, obliging Major van Houten to do the same. The Princess withdrew. They gazed out over the lawns, where the gardeners were tending the rhododendrons; the Kaiser's three dachshunds were hunting in the bushes. He insisted the major sample a liqueur, feeling it might brighten the fellow, but declined any himself. He never touched liqueurs, nor whisky, though he liked to see others doing it. It was almost time for his afternoon nap.

He laid his good hand upon the major's shoulder, gripping it. Even at eighty, his grip was enough to make men wince, but the major he gripped reassuringly. 'You must let me know if there is anything I can do. You have family I can help, perhaps? I provide for more than fifty relatives of my own, so one family more would make little difference. And you yourself. You must let me know what happens. I fancy I may still have influence with the German authorities, if necessary.'

Major van Houten inclined his head. 'Your Highness is most kind.'

The Kaiser patted him. 'Cheer up, my good fellow.'

The major continued to stare at the rhododendrons. Tears stood in his eyes again. 'Forgive me, your Highness. It is the shame of occupation and defeat.'

'I know, I know – knew – those feelings only too well, major.' He paused, then recollected himself. 'But you must brace up, as my English family would say, and face it like a good' – he almost said 'German' – 'soldier.' He let go of the major, finished his coffee and dabbed his lips once more with his napkin. 'And now I must have my nap.'

TWO

At the gatehouse Untersturmführer Martin Krebbs ensured that his platoon was satisfactorily disposed before opening his ration pack for lunch. One section was escorting the Dutch guard back to their barracks, one had taken over the guard duties and the others were eating their rations after sorting out bunks and bedding and cleaning the lodge. The Dutch soldiers had not left it in a bad condition – as the filthy French would have, judging by what he had seen of their quarters during the push through France – but it was not up to Wehrmacht, let alone Schutzstaffel, standards.

He looked again at Huis Doorn. His orders were not to interfere with the old Kaiser but to heed his summons, if any came, and to report back anything that was said. SS Standartenführer Kaltzbrunner, his SS colonel, would interview the Kaiser himself in due course and report to Berlin on his attitudes. Berlin would then decide what to do with the old man. Krebbs's job, meanwhile, was to ensure that the Kaiser did not stray or fall into enemy hands, and to see that no unauthorised personnel were permitted contact with him. Unfortunately, no one had yet provided him with categories of authorisation and he was not even sure whether Major van Houten would now count as an authorised person. It was with some misgivings, therefore, that he had permitted the Dutchman to accept the farewell lunch invitation. He could not check with Standartenführer Kaltzbrunner because the telephone lines were still down and, though he should have been issued with a radio, radios at platoon level in the Wehrmacht had become mysteriously scarce during recent weeks. He made a note in his black pocket book to raise the question again at the next briefing.

Although no palace, Huis Doorn was far larger than any private house that Krebbs had been in. It had four storeys, large windows, a good slate roof, a substantial front door and regular gables. He liked its symmetry – he always liked symmetry – and thought it the sort of house that he would have if he were rich. The Kaiser, it was well known, was exceedingly rich. Despite all the impoverishment of the German people following the Supreme Warlord's misconduct of the last war, he had kept his fortune, living abroad in evident comfort. Meanwhile, honest men who had fought and suffered, such as Krebbs's father, had struggled to bring up a family on the pittance a carpenter earned in Germany in the 1920s, hampered all the time by his gas-damaged lungs. He had died three years before of TB, a death made yet more horrible than it might have been by those weakened lungs. It had been left to Krebbs to support his younger sister and their mother. Well, fortunately, he had been up to the challenge and now they could feel proud to have a son in Schutzstaffel. And he had reason for pride in himself: already he had seen more action than many senior officers. First, he had taken part in the subjugation of Poland with Germany's Russian allies who, though they might not be trustworthy in other ways, were at least sound where the Poles were concerned; secondly, he had then had the good fortune to take part in the invasion of France and had seen real fighting during the advance to Dunkirk. The French and British would have good cause to remember the SS Totenkopf – Death's Head – division. A pity many of the enemy had escaped across the sea, though gratifying numbers had not.

Thinking of this inevitably reminded him of that other business that had happened at the same time, the massacre of the English prisoners at the farm near Le Paradis. It was not his fault, not his doing, but the memory of those sprawling bodies heaped behind the barn was sawdust in his mouth, spoiling the taste of everything he recalled from that period. Not that his other memories were the luxuriating sort he liked to pick over and chew in quiet moments, though there was nothing to be ashamed of in them, either. Most vivid was the afternoon trapped in that bitter, hot little gully with the lead company, thirsty, exhausted, sweating in their uniforms, the screams of the wounded mingling with the shouted commands, the thumps and shocks of mortars and shells, the hateful whine of shrapnel, the spiteful whipcracks of bullets, the stink of cordite and shit. This was all too vivid if he let himself dwell on it, as was his own confusion and fear when he realised they were trapped. There was the first numbing shock of not knowing what to do next, no orders, no procedure to follow, no way forward, no way back. Then there was the sight of troopers from another company fleeing in panic, and the sickening certainty that something had gone suddenly, horribly, irreversibly wrong. Everything in life had made sense until that dry, unexpected afternoon; things had followed on one to another, everything seemed to be leading somewhere until now, incredibly, it was as if it were all about to end in that ridiculous little gully. It was unreasonable, absurd. It could not, surely, end in this squalid, insignificant bit of turf, fit only for sheep to die in, not for him. Yet while it seemed it might, he had been reduced to a waking trance, aware of everything but incapable of anything. Along with his soldiers, he had simply lain there, numbed and paralysed, until the breakout, made by troops to their right, when all had been well again. Except, afterwards, for those English prisoners.

Krebbs was lifted from these memories by the sight of a young woman – a maidservant to judge by her dress and apron – who had come round from the back of the house and was walking down the drive towards them. His soldiers had noticed her and were already making remarks. For him there had been neither time nor opportunity for girls since Renate in Munich. The Polish girls were pretty – those Slavic cheekbones – but full of hate and fear. In France he had seen hardly any, his unit having fought its way through woods and fields while others had the less arduous task of relieving towns and villages that were quickly surrendered, like Paris itself. He had heard, though, that the French girls were more available than the Polish. As for these Dutch, it was early days – he had yet to get near enough one to speak – but there had been that encouraging vision in the orchard, a tall blonde beauty carrying a basket who had stood her ground and stared as the soldiers in the back of the lorry whistled and waved.

He glanced at himself in the full-length mirror he had had fitted to the wall around the corner from the guardroom door so that the guards could check that they were always properly turned-out. Briefly, surreptitiously, he approved his own reflection: his field grey uniform was smart despite campaigning, his boots respectable, his chiselled features clear and fit-looking. Since the invasion of Poland the Führer himself had adopted the grey tunic of the Waffen SS, which was essentially the Wehrmacht uniform but with the eagle and swastika prominent on its left sleeve. The collar of Krebbs's tunic, however, bore not only his rank insignia but his Totenkopf divisional symbol, the silently eloquent Death's Head. He could never see it, on himself or anyone else, without a tremor of pride. Death to the enemy, unsparing unto death of oneself; this was what it meant to be in the Waffen SS, the Führer's Praetorian guard, the shock troops of first and last resort. With luck, there would be time for a run later that afternoon. It was paradoxical that war, for which you trained so hard, should make it difficult to maintain an acceptable fitness routine.

The girl, meanwhile – no tall blonde beauty – nevertheless looked trim and shapely enough as she approached. He would talk to her himself, even though she were only a servant. She might have useful intelligence on the Kaiser's attitudes and on how things were in the household which he could report back to Colonel Kaltzbrunner. Also, she might know when the Dutch major could be expected to return from lunch. He remained anxious about that.

He walked unhurriedly up the gravel path towards the maid, his hands clasped behind his back, staring as a policeman might stare at a citizen he was about to challenge. At first she looked straight back at him but as they closed she lowered her eyes. He approved the clean smartness of her apron and dress, the smoothness of her dark hair, parted in the middle of her submissively bowed head and neatly gathered into a tight bun. He imagined her letting it slowly down while seated at a candle-lit dressing table.

She dispersed his fantasy by looking up, her grey eyes betraying neither nervousness nor any hint of flirtation. Her eyebrows were dark and even, her lips and teeth regular, her skin smooth and slightly tanned. She was older than him, he guessed; late twenties, perhaps even thirty. He had to resist the impulse to click heels and bow, as one did to ladies, since she was only a servant and his soldiers would mock him among themselves.

'Herr Offizier,' she said, before he could address her. 'His Royal Highness and Princess Hermine hope you will be free to join them for dinner this evening.'

His Royal Highness was Highness no longer and should be addressed merely as Prince Wilhelm, as he had been before he succeeded to the throne. The briefing had been strict on that. Clearly, things were different in the household, but Krebbs let it pass. He should not accept this invitation without permission, he thought, as he looked at her.

'Please thank them for the invitation and say I am pleased to accept.' There was time to seek permission and if he had to turn them down, well, so be it. The thing now was to keep her talking. 'If you have a moment, Fräulein, there are some questions I must ask.' He turned off the path and began walking slowly towards the moat, at a slight angle to the house and away from the gatehouse. The short grass had dried off and he could feel the sun on his uniformed shoulders. It was a bright, cheerful day, with blue sky and puffy white clouds. As he had hoped, she fell in alongside him. 'My questions concern the attitudes of Prince Wilhelm and Princess Hermine and those of their German staff towards the Third Reich in Germany, and also their attitudes concerning the occupation of The Netherlands. Also, whether they have had any contact with enemy powers or with powers sympathetic to the enemy.'

'I am new to His Highness's staff, Herr Offizier, and I have no intimate knowledge of Their Highnesses' attitudes, nor of the attitudes of the Germans who are here with them. My position is a junior one.'

Her voice was quiet and low, which he liked, and her German flawless, her diction almost too precise. He liked that, too. 'You are Dutch?'

'Yes, from Friesland. Fries is my first language.'

22

'Has Prince Wilhelm ever, in your hearing, said anything about Herr Hitler, or the Nazi Party or the Third Reich?'

'Here in Huis Doorn Their Highnesses keep what is called Doorn Law, according to which it is not permitted to discuss the new German government.'

'What does he say about England?'

She was looking straight ahead at the narrow bridge across the moat, to the side of the house. There were ducks and water lilies. 'He says that England has always caused him trouble because his mother was English and because many German people thought he was too much in favour of the English and because it is well known that Queen Victoria died in his arms. But the English did not trust him either because they thought he was too German.'

'That is true about the Queen Victoria?'

'He says it was in his arm, his good arm. He sat without moving for two and a half hours. "She softly passed away in my arms," he says. But of England now, he says it is run by Jews and freemasons and is part of the conspiracy of international capital to encircle Germany.'

Krebbs nodded. She was evidently a willing source. He would be justified in seeing more of her. 'It is good that he says that, not only because it is correct but because it is good for him. And the Princess?'

'I have never heard the Princess speak of England. But the old Empress, Princess Dona, is said to have hated the English.'

'Does the Princess say anything of Germany?'

'I believe she admires Herr Hitler and thinks he has done many good things for the German people.'

Such ready co-operation could be either genuine, or naive, or a front. Her answers fitted each. Similarly, her apparent lack of resentment of him, the representative of the invader, was either encouraging or something more sinister.

As they approached the moat some of the ducks waddled towards them, quacking. 'His Highness feeds them every day,' she said. 'It is part of his routine, like sawing and chopping wood.'

There was sudden barking behind them as Arno bounded across the lawn, his thick black fur raised and his fangs visible. The ducks took fright, splashing and squawking back into the water. For the first time, he thought, she appeared to lack confidence. She stood still as the dog approached.

'Be careful, this is Arno, the Princess's dog. He bites strangers sometimes.' She held up her hand as the dog ran at them, calling his name, but he did not stop.

Krebbs faced the dog, keeping his hands behind his back. He was confident with dogs, proud that they respected his authority. He particularly liked German Shepherds, beautiful, strong, loyal dogs. Anyway, he had already made friends with Arno at the gate lodge. Arno slowed as he neared them, barking still, his hackles up. This was a warning, not an attack. Krebbs could tell.

'Arno, sit,' he said quietly. The dog stopped, uncertain and growling. Krebbs held out the back of his hand. 'Arno, come.' The dog advanced warily and sniffed the back of his hand. Its hackles went down and it wagged its tail slowly. Krebbs carefully fondled its head, then held out his hand, palm down, above it. 'Arno, sit.' Arno sat. Krebbs sensed the maid relax behind him.

'You must be good with dogs. Normally, Arno heeds no one but the Princess.'

'You do not like them?'

'Some dogs, but not Arno. He does not like me. I can tell.'

'It must be something he senses about you, perhaps that you are frightened. They sense fear.'

'Maybe.' She resumed walking parallel with the moat, heading for the rear of the house.

Krebbs tapped his thigh for Arno to come to heel and continued beside her. The dog obeyed. 'Also Jews,' he said. 'Some, especially these Shepherds, can sense Jews.'

'Is that so?'

'Probably by their smell.'

He did not want to go any nearer the house, not yet. He stopped. 'I must see to the guard. Will you be serving at dinner this evening?'

'I don't know. It depends who else is on duty.'

'It would be best if people do not know the subject of our conversation.' She said nothing. Her silence and self-containment made him uneasy. 'What is your name?'

'Akki.' She added no other.

'My name is Martin. Untersturmführer Martin Krebbs. I am from Leipzig.' She said nothing. The ducks milled about on the moat while Arno sat at Krebbs's heel. 'I hope you do not feel too badly about the occupation of your country. It is necessary because of our enemies but it is not ill-intentioned.' He spoke rapidly, his words unplanned. She gazed into the moat. He observed the turn of her neck and the profile of her cheek with his eyes but felt them in his chest, as if he had been hit. 'While I am here I shall try to make it all right for you.' It was foolish, unnecessary, wrong, he knew; but he wanted her to react to him.

She glanced at him, still saying nothing, then turned and headed for the house. Arno went to follow but Krebbs tapped his thigh and led him back to the gatehouse.

Major van Houten returned from lunch not very long after, to Krebbs's relief. He seemed sober but said little. Krebbs decided to escort him to the barracks himself. It was some distance away but the lorry that had taken the Dutch soldiers there had returned with those of his own he had sent to escort them. Motor transport was something else that had become mysteriously scarce of late, at platoon

25

and company level, anyway. Perhaps, with the continent all but conquered, the High Command was considering opening another front, such as the invasion of England, so long overdue. That would be harder fighting than anything they had yet faced, if Le Paradis were anything to go by, though the pathetic little English army was now much depleted even allowing for those that had escaped from Dunkirk, and its equipment was anyway inferior. But they would be bitter, the English, if they ever found out about Paradis.

Meanwhile, the Dutch major showed no sign of wanting to flee – indeed, he had had his chance over lunch – and permitted himself to be relieved of his side arm without demur. He answered questions put to him, volunteered nothing and seemed perfectly correct, although his imperturbable, doleful manner made it impossible to tell what he was thinking, and therefore what he might do. Krebbs disliked ambiguity and uncertainty, and wanted to be rid of him. He also disliked the driver of the lorry, an unfortunately all too typical representative of the transport platoon of the Wehrmacht battalion to which he was attached. The drivers appeared to regard their vehicles as their own and gave the impression that transporting soldiers was at best a favour, at worst an imposition. Not that the driver said anything, of course, but his expression on realising that he would have to bring Krebbs back after dropping off the major and so miss the HQ company meal was eloquent enough for Krebbs to consider a charge of dumb insolence. However, there were plenty of other things to be doing and he did not want to miss his own dinner because of the formalities of disciplinary action. The driver turned the lorry round and sat with the engine idling. Krebbs left Arno with the guard, telling them not to feed him. German Shepherds had to be kept in good shape.

*   *   *

26

Princess Hermine sat before her ornate dressing-table mirror, contemplating the ruin of her face. Hair one could do something with, other bits could be covered up, but the sagging and wrinkling of the face, the drawing-down of the lips, the stretching and pouching of the cheeks, the awful, daily collapse of an entire landscape was saddening beyond words. Why could not God have made an exception of the face? Let everything else age, let it all go, but keep the face young, or at least presentable. The worst thing was that the wrinkles showed most when she smiled. Yet she liked to smile, when appropriate. In youth, her smile had been a great asset; it would be hard to give it up now.

She touched her wiry hair a few more times with the delicate silver brush, part of her wedding present from Willie. Her blue dress with white silk lower sleeves would do for dinner, along with a single string of pearls. It would be sensible not to be too ostentatious and anyway it was not as if their guest were important in himself, only for what he represented. It was essential that he should report back – surely he would report – on a modest and well-disposed household. After all, if one could not keep one's face one could at least take some satisfaction from one's achievements, and nurture one's ambitions.

As for achievements, she had not done badly. First, she had escaped her family. The Poison Squirt, as her sisters used to call her, had stunned them all with her rich and successful first marriage and then her five children, bang, bang, bang, like peas from a pod. Then came her comfortable widowhood and everyone had assumed that was it with her until, bang, she had stunned them again – stunned them speechless – with her marriage to the widowed Kaiser. What did it matter that he preserved Dona's room as a shrine, with only himself and the cleaning maids allowed in while she, the Princess, had to make do with lesser rooms? And what though he spent hours in Dona's rose garden, in contemplation and prayer? He was so obviously glad not to be alone, so grateful to her for marrying him, so fond of her and so generous, always giving her things.

Only on one important subject did they differ, and that was submerged most of the time. This was the question of striving for a Hohenzollern restoration, the Kaiser's triumphant return to Germany as its king once more. It was quite obvious that Germany needed royal leadership to counter-balance this regime of corporals and tobacconists. Not only to counter-balance, but to complement and complete. They were not doing badly, these Nazis, and one could have much sympathy with them; in many ways they were right, and certainly they were doing well with this war. But they needed guidance, wisdom and experience, someone who could ensure the allegiance of the armed forces and the aristocracy. Naturally, there was only one who could do that.

The problem was Willie, not because he was against returning to his rightful throne – on the contrary, it was the very thing that, deep down, he most longed for. Of that she was sure. However, he could not acknowledge it fully, it was too delicate, rejection would be too wounding, worse than the original exile and more final. Therefore, his Princess must take soundings for him and prepare the way. Not for herself, of course. It made no difference to her whether she became Empress of Germany – though her sisters, yes, imagine what they would say – but she would do it for his sake. It would mean so much to him. So, it was important to be nice to these Nazis, especially now that they were here in Holland and, as always, had it in their power to continue or refuse Willie's financial allowance. Again, if one could not keep one's face, one could at least keep one's head and perhaps do the state, and dear Willie, some service.

The Princess left her room. The door to Dona's sanctuary was shut, as always, but Schulz, Willie's valet, was creeping along the corridor in his usual funereal manner, his face irritatingly expressionless, as if he were aware of no one or nothing. In fact, he noticed everything and was treasured by Willie for his 'unfathomable discretion'.

'Is His Majesty in the late Empress's room?' she asked.

Schulz looked absurdly surprised, as if the wall had addressed him. 'No, your Highness.'

'Do you know where he is?'

'Yes, your Highness.'

'Perhaps you would be so kind as to tell me.'

'He is in the rose garden, your Highness.'

She looked out from a window and saw him, on a bench, bareheaded, his stick between his knees. He had a better head of hair than many men half his age, albeit that it was silver now, like his beard. The three dachshunds, ridiculous creatures, were playing nearby. The roses were like a red sea around him. For a moment it reminded her of a sea of poppies, the sort of thing the English had made such a fuss about since the last war. Willie was wearing his field grey uniform, the one he had worn at their wedding. That was a good sign; it showed he meant to impress by being businesslike, not just showy. He often wore uniforms in the evenings, normally more elaborate than this. He had a ridiculous number – over three hundred German alone, plus Russian, Austrian, Portuguese, Swedish, Danish and English. She had once remarked to him that if they became poor he could sell his uniforms to the various armies and navies to help them all keep the war going.

Field grey was also a good choice because it showed solidarity with the Wehrmacht and with the Nazi attempts to create a new, more egalitarian, social order. She hoped he would not wear his medals, but if he did – well, probably no one nowadays remembered that he had never won or earned any of them. It was doubtful that he any longer acknowledged that even to himself. Anyway, medals might impress the young Untersturmführer. Willie must – would – be king again. She went down to the rose garden to be with him.

THREE

Krebbs was anxious before and during dinner, though not because of his table manners. He had learned those on becoming an officer and, although this table was more a minefield than most – more dishes and implements and the danger of arcane customs he had never heard of – he felt protected by his status. Not only because of his commissioned rank, but because his SS insignia guaranteed immediate recognition and respect wherever he went. It did not guarantee liking, but – like him or loathe him – no one could ignore a representative of the SS.

Whether or not he was liked nevertheless did make a difference to Martin Krebbs and he generally tried to render himself likeable. His first cause of anxiety had been whether he would get to the dinner at all. He had arrived at the barracks with Major van Houten that afternoon to find battalion headquarters in confusion. A few hours, he was learning, could be a long time in war. He had left an organised, efficient unit that morning, one that was grateful after weeks in the field to have the luxury of proper barracks and an attractive part of Holland to occupy. Arrangements were being made to accommodate

Dutch Army prisoners, pending High Command decisions as to what should happen to them. Krebbs and his new friend, Stefan – a Wehrmacht Oberleutnant who had displayed none of the stand-offishness of the other officers in the Wehrmacht unit to which Krebbs was attached – had even secured a room to themselves.

But when he arrived with the major late that afternoon he found the battalion dispersed. Headquarters was still there but the commanding officer was away at a senior officers' briefing. Only headquarters company was still in residence, functioning as guard and administrator, the others having been hurriedly deployed many kilometres away in some undefined coastal defence role, allegedly temporary. The second-in-command had gone with them, taking most of the remaining transport. There were rations only for the headquarters company and now, suddenly, many more Dutch prisoners than anticipated. No one had any idea how long they were to be kept, whether it was permissible to disperse them to their homes, whether they were to be set to work, or what. Everyone was appealing to Hauptmann Buff, the harassed adjutant, who had neither the authority to make decisions about such matters nor any guidance from higher formations, who were preoccupied with their own problems. The quartermaster had taken the room that Krebbs and Stefan had found for themselves.

The parade ground was crowded with disarmed Dutch soldiers, sitting, talking, smoking or simply standing in surly groups. They were not men who had been defeated in battle; there had been some fighting – one or two Dutch units had fought well – but most Dutch soldiers had not fought. They had been ordered by their officers to surrender in the face of the overwhelming force that had swept across their country like the North Sea breaking in to their beloved polders. Surrender doubtless bred both relief and resentment. Krebbs told the lorry driver to park at the edge of the parade ground and be ready to return with him and his escorting soldiers within twenty minutes. He told Major van Houten to wait while he asked where, or to whom, to consign him.

The major glanced at his several hundred morose compatriots who, though unarmed, could easily have overpowered their captors. His long face was as lugubrious as ever but something in his eyes suggested the nearest Krebbs had seen to a smile. 'Don't bet your pay-packet on getting an answer, Herr Leutnant,' he said, calling Krebbs by his Wehrmacht equivalent rank.

Krebbs had left the barracks early that day in good spirits, having been told that guarding the Kaiser was an important task which the High Command wished to be performed by Wehrmacht troops under command of an SS officer. It appeared he would combine the advantages of having his own independent daytime command with the comfort of good barrack accommodation at night. Now, however, guarding the Kaiser seemed the last, and least, thing on anyone's mind. The adjutant's office was crowded with supplicants and applicants, while engineers squeezed in and out testing telephones and laying new lines. Everyone was talking and at first no one heeded Krebbs's clicked heels and crisp 'Heil Hitler!' salute at the door. He always made a point of that rather than the traditional army salute.

Hauptmann Buff half raised one hand, holding a cigarette, but without getting out of his chair and without interrupting his questioning of an engineer. When he had finished with the man he looked up at Krebbs with weary eyes. 'What are you doing here?'

Krebbs explained.

'Feed him to the birds, if you like,' the adjutant interrupted. 'You can see what it's like here. We've been made a collection point for Dutch armed forces throughout the province, only no one told us. At the same time all four rifle companies have been detached to coastal protection in case of English raids and I've been left with the remnants of HQ company to do everything. Just be grateful you're not here. I should stay at Doorn if I were you and keep your head down. If the old man wants you to have dinner with him, eat it. There's bound to be more of it than anyone will get here. Meanwhile, just make sure no unauthorised persons approach him and that he doesn't make a bolt for it or do anything stupid. Note anything important he says or does so you've got something to report to your SS Standartenführer, your colonel – what's his name? – Kaltzbrunner.' He pronounced the name with careful distinction. 'As for your Dutch major, tell him if he's got any food in his pocket he should eat it now, before anyone else does. Then make yourself scarce before I find you something to do. Heil Hitler.' He put the cigarette in his mouth.

There was an ironic edge to the adjutant's dismissal that took Krebbs aback. It suggested an attitude corrosive of discipline and endeavour, the sort of thing for which he had seen men sacked from Braunschweig, the SS officer academy. SS personnel were supposed to report such instances; he would remember it. He went off to retrieve his kit from the room that was now part of the quartermaster's ample suite of offices, then returned to find Major van Houten standing smoking by the lorry. Nobody, anywhere, guards or prisoners, seemed to have any idea what to do. Everyone was standing and staring at everyone else. There was no tension, no expectation, only a depressed waiting. There was not even a football.

'Your driver, Herr Leutnant, may have gone absent without leave,' said the major. 'As soon as you left he said he was going to the toilet and he has not reappeared. Your escort – my escort – are catching up on doubtless well-deserved sleep in the back. It may be possible to find and reprimand your driver in this sad situation but it would take some time and meanwhile someone might commandeer your lorry. If I were you, Herr Leutnant, and speaking as one officer to another' – the major's expression gave nothing away but the exaggerated lowering of his voice suggested humour – 'I would take your lorry and your men and go, quickly. In all armies it is the same: you are either doing something, or something is done to you.' He transferred his cigarette to his other hand and took a key from his tunic pocket. 'I took the precaution of relieving your driver of his ignition key. I hope you don't object to a German soldier taking orders from an enemy officer. If you do, you can add it to his charge sheet.'

Krebbs had never driven a car, let alone a lorry. Nor, he knew, had any of his men. Finding the driver and then dealing with him would certainly take time. He might not get back for dinner with the Kaiser. He was as determined not to let that happen as he had been about anything in life, except perhaps getting his commission. It was essential, he told himself – and would have protested to anyone who asked – that this first move of the Kaiser's should be accepted. It was important to the Reich to have a co-operative and approving, or at least acquiescent, Kaiser in exile. Neutral countries would be impressed by that, just as they would be impressed the other way if the Kaiser defected to England or somewhere – well, it would have to be to England or its empire, since there was no other enemy left to fight now. But behind all his reasoning, like sunlight filtered through leaves, was the pleasing image of the maidservant. He had persuaded himself that she would be there; and if she would, he would, even though she was only a servant.

'Can you drive?' he asked.

Major van Houten's eyebrows arched. 'I am a qualified army instructor.'

'Would you be so good as to drive us back?'

'If that is an invitation to co-operate with the invader, it would be treasonable to comply. But if it is an order from a captor to his prisoner-of-war, it would be correct.'

Krebbs permitted himself a smile. 'It is an order, Herr Major.'

The major drove the unfamiliar lorry better than its Wehrmacht driver, with less grating of gears and less bumping and jerking. The noise in the cab made conversation difficult, which suited Krebbs because he wanted to think. At least, that was what he told himself but now that he had the opportunity he found nothing on which he wanted, mentally, to dwell. He wanted neither to recall the past nor – his more usual state – to fantasise about a glorious future. He felt he was somehow floating in no-man's land, seeking nothing, imagining nothing. It was a novel state, but not unsettling. As they approached the tall trees of Doorn the major turned to him. 'I am sure you will take good care of your charge, Herr Leutnant, but there is one small piece of advice I should like to offer, if it is permitted.'

'It is permitted.' Krebbs was beginning to feel he could like the man, despite his being an enemy.

'Be respectful of him. He is half a genius and half a child. He is clever but not always wise. He has great inner youth, he is much younger than his years. He has never properly grown up but he has much valuable experience. He is not tactful but he is sensitive. Listen to him, put up with him, and you can learn, as I did.'

'So, what can I learn from the old man?'

'You can learn' – the major paused while he turned at the village crossroads towards the gate lodge, going hand over hand on the heavy wheel and changing down with an adroit double-clutch movement – 'you can learn from his wrongness. When he is most wrong, you learn most.'

'He is often wrong, then?'

'He is at least half wrong, always. It is his nature. But he is also half right and not always how you expect.'

Now, sitting at dinner, they were all listening respectfully as the Kaiser described his archaeological discoveries on Corfu. Archaeology had become his passion and his mottled old face became animated as he spoke, heedless of the breadcrumbs in his pointed white beard. He had founded and now annually hosted the Doorn Research Society, a symposium. He should, Krebbs thought as he halved his last piece of cold meat, to make it seem more, have been a professor, not an emperor. That was where his true gifts lay. Krebbs was not sure where Corfu was, though he was increasingly sure that he had been wrong to let Major van Houten drive himself back to the barracks, unescorted. It was all very well accepting the major's argument that, since his family lived in the officers' quarters beside the barracks, there was nowhere else he would be tempted to go. He knew, too, that the lorry had not enough fuel to get much farther. It would be all right, most probably, but it still would not look good in an inquiry if it were not. It was wrong, whatever his reasons. He had made the decision hurriedly, in order not to be late for dinner, and now the girl was not there. Perhaps she had the night off. Perhaps she had a boyfriend. Apparently the Kaiser nearly always had cold meat in the evenings.

Apart from the Kaiser and the Princess, dinner comprised only himself and the Kaiser's private secretary, von Islemann, with his Dutch wife. Von Islemann was pale, exact, polite and unforthcoming. He had been with the Kaiser since before his exile and was reputedly devoted to him. He was certainly too loyal, Krebbs felt, to be pumped on his master. Also, he probably thought too well of his own aristocratic background, and too little of Krebbs's, to form anything like common cause, unless under the pressure of events. Nothing he said betrayed any indication of his attitude towards the Reich. His Dutch wife seemed a pleasant, easy-going, practical sort of woman, a daughter of the household at Amerongen where the Kaiser had spent his first few years in exile. She talked about the tulip-growing areas of Holland and their contribution to the economy, as well as about Leipzig, Krebbs's home town. No one mentioned the occupation. Krebbs was surprised that the Kaiser wore field grey; he had assumed he could afford something more elaborate and special.

'And what does Herr Hitler propose now?' asked Princess Hermine. 'He carries all before him so expeditiously. Will he stop here?'

It was a moment before Krebbs realised she was addressing him. He put down his fork. 'I regret, Princess, that I am not privy to the Führer's plans. Once we have made the coastline of Europe properly secure, I imagine we shall prepare to deal with England.'

The Princess smiled encouragement. 'Certainly, logically, it must be the next thing to do.'

The china rattled as the Kaiser struck the table with his good right arm. 'It is not only logical, it is a necessity – *the* necessity if we are to save European civilisation for the world. We must free England from the Jews and the freemasons and the capital that is corrupting her. Then we must establish a European customs union and a European currency as I have been urging for more than forty years and show the world what a Christian civilisation means. For forty years have I been urging Juda-England to decide whether she is with Europe or America but now the time has come to decide for her, since she cannot make up her own mind. Your Führer' – he looked portentously at Krebbs, as if pronouncing weighty judgement – 'does well.'

During the pause that followed von Islemann murmured, 'Heil Hitler'. It was impossible to tell whether he was serious or mocking.

The Kaiser got stiffly to his feet and raised his glass of sparkling red wine. 'To Germany. May God protect her and save her from encirclement.'

They stood and toasted. As they sat Krebbs caught his holster on the arm of the chair. He shifted his belt a fraction, with a creaking of leather. He alone had come armed to the table. No one had said anything, of course, but he felt awkward despite the enhanced sense of importance and the thrill of potency that bearing arms always conferred.

After dinner the ladies withdrew to Princess Hermine's sitting-room and the men to the Kaiser's smoking-room where, in studded leather armchairs beneath the dominating portrait of Frederick the Great, they took liqueurs and cigars. Krebbs was served last, which enabled him to follow von Islemann in choosing whisky. The Kaiser had only coffee, but they all had cigars.

The Kaiser continued to talk about archaeological digs on Corfu, with von Islemann making informed comments. Krebbs said nothing. In one respect it had been a satisfactory evening: he had something to report on the Kaiser's attitude towards the Reich. Such a report, particularly as it would be the first, might go all the way to the top, especially if it were favourable. He had learned already that favourable reports gained higher and wider circulation than unfavourable, and brought more credit to their originators. Of course, the Kaiser's remarks and toasts could simply have been for Krebbs's benefit in an attempt to ensure that the Reich would continue paying the royal allowance, now possibly in jeopardy because the Kaiser was technically no longer in exile but in German-controlled territory. Krebbs could imagine Colonel Kaltzbrunner taking that line. It would be best, therefore, if he said it himself, in his report, thus getting credit for that, too. He felt he was learning the ways of bureaucracy.

He sipped his whisky, matching von Islemann sip for sip. It was very good whisky, better than any he had tasted. Several times the Kaiser interrupted his own monologue in order to re-light his cigar. Krebbs enjoyed his cigar, too. It was mild and flavour-full but not hot, like cheaper ones. Who would have thought that he, a carpenter's son who might never have left Leipzig, would one day sit with the Kaiser, drinking his whisky, smoking his cigars and talking after dinner? It could never have happened without National Socialism. His father, loyal soldier of the Kaiser, would have been proud. He would write to his mother about it. He accepted more whisky, and then more.

Von Islemann was leaving. Perhaps they all were. Krebbs was struggling to get out of his armchair with cigar and whisky in hand when the Kaiser, who had remained seated, waved him down. 'It is not necessary for you to leave, Untersturmführer. You can stay. We can talk.'

Krebbs settled back, shifting several times because his holstered pistol was digging in to him again. He felt very slightly dizzy, and blamed the cigar.

'You would like some more whisky?' asked the Kaiser.

'No, thank you, your Highness.' He was supposed, of course, to address the old man as 'sir' or 'Prince Wilhelm'. To call him 'your Highness' implied recognition of him as emperor, which he no longer was. But it was awkward when everyone else around him used the term, especially as the Kaiser had just accorded him his SS rank rather than its Wehrmacht equivalent. Now that they were alone, Krebbs felt easier about doing what the Kaiser expected.

'Some more water, perhaps?'

'Please, thank you, your Highness.'

'I drink mainly water. I do not abide whisky.' The

Kaiser pressed the servant bell. 'Tell me about your life, Untersturmführer. Was your father in the war?'

The Kaiser was interested in Krebbs's father's war service, asking many questions, and Krebbs talked freely. When Krebbs described how his father had won his Iron Cross during Operation Michael, the 1918 Spring Offensive, the Kaiser held up his hand.

'I, too, have the Iron Cross. Would you like to see it?'

'Thank you, your Highness, I should like to very much.'

The Kaiser gave orders to someone evidently standing just behind Krebbs, out of sight. Krebbs did not turn to look, feeling it better to stay still. He had let his cigar go out and had ceased to sip his whisky. The man behind him said something and left the room.

Afterwards, Krebbs convinced himself he had sensed her presence before he saw her. It wasn't only the rustle of her skirts when she came in bearing the medal on a cushion but a change in the atmosphere of the room, felt as a sensation on the back of his neck and head, like a passing ray of heat. Still he did not turn but watched her come into view carrying the small purple cushion with both hands. She knelt deftly before the Kaiser to show it to him, her tightly-pinned dark hair shining beneath the candelabra. The Kaiser took his medal and indicated that she should put the cushion on the round table before them. She straightened and did so, then stood by with her hands clasped before her. Krebbs sought to catch her eye but her head was bowed. The light fell now on her cheeks, forehead and eyelids. He gazed at the dark arches of her eyebrows.

With his good hand, the Kaiser held out his medal to Krebbs. 'The Iron Cross, First Class,' he said, reverentially.

Krebbs took it. His father's was Second Class. The other difference was that his father's was earned. It was well

41

known that the great Warlord of the Second Reich had never fired a shot in anger, or been shot at, or mined, or shelled. Or gassed. Krebbs handed it back, saying nothing.

'I have many other medals and honours,' said the Kaiser. His watery blue eyes opened wide, as in astonishment at his own achievement. 'And I have many, many uniforms, German and foreign. I will show you my uniforms. Come.' He got to his feet, laid his medal on the cushion, and walked, slow and upright, towards the door, his cigar propped in his unmoving left hand. Unburdened by cigar and whisky, Krebbs left his own chair with reasonable ease this time and stood with arm outstretched, indicating that the girl should precede him, though it was not clear that the invitation had included her. He raised his eyebrows and smiled. She glanced at him without smiling, picked up the cushion and medal and, with a further faint rustle of her skirts, followed the old man.

They walked in silent procession into the corridor outside the Kaiser's study. The corridor was lined with books and had a desk and telephone by the study door. From there they went past the stairs and through a large sitting-room to a high, closed door. The Kaiser's cigar left a thin, vanishing trail of smoke behind him. The girl followed, holding the cushion before her like a crown. Krebbs watched the hem of her black dress as it brushed and swayed against door-jambs and banisters. Once, it lingered on the back of a sofa like a surreptitious caress. He could hear the creaking of his own leather boots and belt. There was no dizziness now, just a little light-headedness. He felt confident that something good was going to happen. An ornate mantel clock tinkled ten as they passed. The rest of the house was already silent.

The Kaiser paused at the door and addressed Krebbs over the head of the girl. 'You will never have seen so many beautiful uniforms. All are mine.'

He turned on the electric light, leading them into a long, high, yellow-patterned room with floor-to-ceiling windows and drawn, heavy gold curtains. High up were pictures of princes and generals, though this time Frederick the Great's usual dominance was shared with Frederick III, the Kaiser's father. Throughout the room, on long wooden hangers, were hundreds of uniforms in black, gold, red, yellow, sky blue, white and shades of green. There was a warm, rich smell of expensive cloth. It was a grove of exotic military plants.

'Is it not splendid?' the Kaiser asked, with a wave of his right hand, in which he once again held his cigar. 'There is nothing like it, anywhere. So many regiments, so many no longer in existence, of course. But if Herr Hitler runs short of uniforms for his soldiers I, the Kaiser, could help him. I could furnish a regiment from here.' He laughed, stroking the epaulettes that adorned a colonel of Tsarist cavalry. He walked slowly between the aisles, touching the uniforms and commenting on them as if everyone shared his passion. He was careful to keep his cigar ash away. The girl followed with the medal on its purple cushion. Krebbs caught her eye once more, again without obvious response, while the Kaiser enumerated the vanished Austro-Hungarian regiments of which he had been honorary colonel.

'They were the best at uniforms, Franz-Joseph and his people. They would be still, there would still be an Austrian Empire if only they had taken my advice.' He stopped, so that they all stood close together. He exhaled smoke in the girl's face while addressing Krebbs. 'Well, at first it was the old man's – Bismarck's – advice. "Run your empire from Hungary," he told them. "Get into the middle of it. Vienna is too small, too remote." I told them so myself, many times. I told Archduke Ferdinand before he was murdered. That was the incident which started the last war, you see, before we expected it. We were dragged into it by Austrian incompetence. If the Archduke had heeded me he would not have been killed.' He laughed and puffed again on his cigar. There were tears of mirth in his eyes. 'You know, Ferdinand, he was so fat, they had to sew him into his uniform. This is why, when he was shot, they could not unbutton him. It was his own fault. I always said to him, I said, "You should be grateful you are not English. They would call you Fatty Ferdie there." He did not like that. Every time I said it, no matter how often, he did not like it.' He laughed again and walked on.

Krebbs waved the smoke from the girl's face with an exaggerated sweep of his arm and a mock bow. This time she smiled.

'And here,' continued the Kaiser, stopping at the top of the next row and tapping another uniform shoulder, 'is my colonelcy of the Imperial Russian Guard, awarded me by the hand of my cousin, the Tsar himself. God rest his soul. What happened to him and his family was terrible, you know. Terrible.' His face was earnest now, almost urgent. 'They butchered them, those Bolsheviks butchered them, the children too, every last one. These are the people who are now your Herr Hitler's closest allies. Out of spite, they did it. Malice. Spite.' He clenched his fist, flattening his cigar between his fingers. 'That is why England must be destroyed. A word from England at that time would have been enough to prevent it. Only amid the ruins of London will I forgive my cousin Georgie, their king. He is the dog who did not bark, when he alone could have. I could do nothing. I had to flee in case my own family suffered the same at the hands of the German Bolsheviks.'

He stared at Krebbs, eyes bulging and the veins in his neck standing out, as if he held Krebbs responsible. The ugly crooked scar on his right cheek looked almost as if it might split. That scar had surprised Krebbs when he was introduced to the Kaiser; it did not appear in any of the pictures. 'Fortunately, Herr Hitler and the Party have solved the problem of German communists now, your Highness,' he said.

The Kaiser considered his cigar for a moment, then dropped it on the polished floor and ground it beneath his boot. 'Yes, that is something.' He carried on down the row.

The girl looked down at the cigar as if considering how, while holding the cushion, she might pick it up. Krebbs swiftly bent and picked it up by its dry end. He raised his eyebrows and stood back for her to proceed. She lowered her head, smiling again, and followed the Kaiser.

He had stopped to hold out the gold-braided sleeve of a dark blue uniform, apparently unaware that they were not yet with him. 'Here, you see, I was also an admiral of the English navy. Not only that, it was I who taught them to salute. When I used to go with my grandmama Queen Victoria and the family to Cowes I noticed their saluting was not only very sloppy but very – very individual, to put it kindly. All sorts of people saluted in so many different ways that you did not know whether they were saluting or waving or had something wrong with them. So I complained. They said it was like that in Nelson's time and they never liked to change anything that was Nelson's. Well, they are eating the fruits of that attitude still, from what I hear. Our submarines will surely bring them to their knees, as we almost did last time.' He laughed again. 'But they gave me a nice desk with Nelson's last signal emblazoned on it. And they standardised their naval saluting. So I won.'

'Your Highness has been a great help to the English,' the girl said quietly.

She spoke as if she were part of the conversation. Her confidence surprised Krebbs. What could she know about the Kaiser and the English, apart from what she had just heard? But the Kaiser reacted as if it were normal for servants to volunteer their opinions. Perhaps he had not noticed which of them spoke.

'Help to the English? Help? I who had to remind them what they were, or should be?' His face was suffused with indignation. 'I who put their Queen into her coffin which I had to have made, I who had to re-harness the horses when they refused to move the bier, I who was in charge at Osborne and got everything moving after she died – the only time, let me tell you, that a German sovereign has ruled over any part of England – I who was cheered through the streets by the English, before they came to hate me? I was their personification, only they did not know it, they have so inadequate a concept of themselves.' He stared in indignant appeal, then resumed more calmly. 'Mind you, the German people is little better. I was what they should be – could have been – only they did not know me. All this was before you were born, of course, either of you.' His mouth worked for a few moments, with no words. 'My God, but it is true they didn't even have a coffin for her. Everyone knew she was dying but their wonderful officials, who are paid to think of these things, hadn't thought of it. I myself went to a ship-builder in Cowes and got him to do it. Think of that. The English can't even bury their sovereigns without Wilhelm. And now look at how they have repaid me.'

Almost shouting, he smote himself on the chest with his clenched fist, staring as if they had affronted him. 'Thanks to the English, I am stuck here having to be nice to this bunch of shirted gangsters who will ruin my country.' He turned to Krebbs. 'Not you. I don't mean you. It is not your fault. But your shirts, your gangsters.' He clasped his weak hand in his good and walked stiffly, but with surprising speed, from the room.

They listened as his footsteps faded in the outer room. Krebbs turned to her. 'Congratulations, Akki, you have provoked a reaction.'

'His Highness is an emotional man.'

'A man of contradictions.'

'Of many sides.'

'Who exactly does he mean by "shirted gangsters", do you think?'

'I think you must know that, Herr Offizier.'

'My name is Martin. I told you that.'

She inclined her head and turned for the door, still carrying the cushion and medal before her. Krebbs followed. He wanted to keep her talking. At the door of the Kaiser's study he stopped. He felt awkward about following her in, though the house was silent and they were surely the only people still up. When she came out she closed the door carefully and made for the stairs. By no sign or gesture did she encourage his attendance, but she did nothing positively to discourage it.

He felt suddenly angry. 'He is a ridiculous old man,' he said, as they went down the stairs. 'Vain and boastful. Who does he think he is? What does he think he is? Does he really believe we are gangsters? He said good things about us at dinner. Stupid.'

She pursed her lips and held up her finger. 'I think he means what he says when he says it,' she said, in a low voice.

'But he says such different things, contradictory things.'

'He means them when he says them, like a child.'

They were almost whispering now. 'So Major van Houten told me, or something like it. He called it "inner youth", this childishness. And that Iron Cross you have just put away. His possession of it and his pride in it are an insult to the men who have earned it. He did nothing to earn any of his medals, apart from being a royal parasite.

Germany is better off without such people. I don't know why we should bother to guard him.'

'Yes, why do you guard him?'

'In case the Dutch people turn against him. It would be bad if the Third Reich could not protect the head of the Second.'

'Why should we Dutch turn against him now? He has been here over twenty years.'

'Well – because of this occupation, perhaps. Because we are here. They – you – some of your people, disaffected elements, might resent us.'

Her expression gave nothing away. 'Is that the only reason?'

'So far as I know, yes. It is enough, I think. Well, perhaps also to make sure he doesn't do anything stupid.'

'What kind of thing?'

He hesitated. Again, he was saying more than he should but being with her made him want to confide. 'Well, I don't know. To make sure he stays here where it is safe, I suppose.'

They had reached the vestibule, which now functioned as a household chapel and was furnished with a lectern and chairs. She switched off the chandelier behind the high, glass-panelled front door. 'What must you do now?' he asked.

'I have to go down to the kitchen and then back upstairs to bed, turning off all the lights and checking the doors as I go.'

'May I see the kitchen?'

'Are you also a food inspector, Untersturmführer?' Her correct use of his SS rank sounded playful. She pronounced it familiarly.

'I have to inspect my soldiers' food, so it is useful to make comparisons.'

He followed her down the narrow stairs that led to the kitchen and domestic offices in the basement. The kitchen was warm, the utensils and copper pots gleamed, the great shallow sinks were scrubbed white. She took off her apron and hung it behind the door. For a moment it looked as if she were going to let down her hair, but she was merely touching it back into place. He did not want to stare too obviously at her, so paced about as if inspecting. His leather-soled, hob-nailed boots sounded gratifyingly authoritative on the stone-flagged floor. 'Are you making some coffee?'

She looked at him with her arms still raised as she touched her hair. 'Is that a request, Herr Untersturmführer?'

'If you please. I also request that you call me Martin when we are alone. I have already mentioned this.'

For the first time she smiled openly. 'Untersturmführer suits you so well. It must be your uniform.'

'Shall I take it off?' She busied herself with the coffee things. He felt he had made a mistake. 'Unfortunately, I do not have my black SS dress uniform to put on in its place.'

Over coffee, sitting at the deal table, she asked him about his family. He then asked about hers, discovering that she was an only child, that her father, a farmer, was dead and that her widowed mother had married a ne'er-do-well and was last heard of in Portugal. She did not even have a current address. They had got on badly since her father died.

'How did you come here?' he asked.

'I heard there were more jobs and better pay in the south of Holland so I took a train to Utrecht and stayed with a girlfriend who was there then and she had heard they were looking for suitable staff to live in here at Doorn. They have been good employers to me, here. We have very nice rooms upstairs and a bathroom, much better rooms than servants usually have.'

He grinned. 'I should like to inspect your room.'

'The Princess is very strict.'

She seemed content to sit and talk, her elbows on the table, her sleeves pushed up to expose her slim forearms, her cup held before her. Her hands were delicate, not housemaid's hands, he thought. He took one in his own.

'You will spoil your hands if you do too much house-work, too much scrubbing. Have you done much housework before? It does not look like it.'

She removed her hand, put down her cup and held up both hands before her, turning them slowly back and forth. 'The secret with hands, as with so many things, is to be careful.' She went to the sink with the cups and saucers.

As he watched her washing up it occurred to him that he could help by drying. It was not a manly thing to do but it might elicit gratitude and make her think he was considerate. On the other hand, she might not respect him for it and, anyway, it was inappropriate for a German officer to do such a thing, especially in uniform. In fact, even to be seen in the kitchen with a serving-girl was to risk ridicule, although he could justify it by the need to get information about the household. But there was also no need to rush the cultivation of this beautiful girl who would surely, one day, give herself to him. She was not going anywhere soon; neither was he, and it was good not to be seen to be too keen.

He was thinking this as she stood drying her hands. He was still thinking it when he pulled her to him and kissed her on the lips. It was abruptly and clumsily done, with her hands and the tea-towel crushed against his chest so that she could not have embraced him even had she wanted.

She remained passive in his arms, neither responding nor turning her head away. Her lips were soft and slack. He let go. She turned and folded the tea-towel over the rail on the front of the oven, her back to him now. It was presumably what she had been about to do when he grabbed her. He wanted to kiss her neck. 'You must go and I must lock the Kaiser's door behind you,' she said.

He felt foolish. 'May I see you again?'

'Of course you will see me again.'

'I mean, like this.' He felt he was abasing himself, but didn't care.

She looked at him solemnly. Then, with the ghost of a smile that never seemed quite to appear, only to disappear, turned towards the stairs. 'It is possible, Untersturmführer, that we might resume our conversation.'

FOUR

Conversation did not resume during the next few days. Krebbs glimpsed her several times in the grounds of the house, carrying bread for the Kaiser, upright and mechanical in his blue serge suit no matter how warm the day, to feed to the ducks; or taking orders from the Princess in the rose garden; or helping set out tables and chairs on the terrace. Once, when Krebbs was returning through the beeches from his early evening run, he saw her walking alone through the arched gatehouse towards the village. He waited vainly for her to return, talking to the guard, needlessly re-inspecting his men's quarters, complaining about the exterior paint-work. When she had not returned by dusk he concluded she must have come back on the footpath that led from the village church, which had its own entrance to the park. He forbore interrogating the sentry there but, the longer he went without another encounter with her, the more determined he became to contrive one.

One morning there were four maids seeing to tables and chairs in the orangery. Their aprons were startlingly white as they moved in and out of the sun and shade, their voices carrying indistinctly through the trees and across the park. He was too far away to tell whether she was one of them, but thought she was. They were laughing about something. So, he thought, occupation is not so terrible after all.

For a week there was no army post, which was bad for the men. Letters from home were important for morale and without them there was a distinct lowering. It was exasperating; they were not in action or in some remote theatre of war but were for the time being a static unit not many kilometres from the German border, almost a home garrison. The driver of the ration lorry said that the post had been delivered to HQ but some idiot in HQ company had sent it all out to the distant rifle companies without sorting it first, so it would probably travel round the whole battalion before getting back to HQ company, then there would be a further delay before it reached Doorn. No one knew where it was now.

That, and the removal of one sick man with suspected appendicitis, was almost the only contact they had with HQ. Krebbs had used the now-working gatehouse telephone to summon transport for the sick man, and even then was made to feel that Doorn was the last place on anyone's mind. HQ never rang them, which in some ways was good, but for an officer who had seen recent action, was keen to see more and had already been commended for his determination and coolness under fire, it was hard not to feel neglected. 'Just keep your head down and enjoy comfort while you've got it,' the adjutant had said again on the phone, though in a more friendly manner this time. 'There's a lot more war to come. You won't miss it, don't worry.'

He also had to keep the men occupied. Once they had thoroughly cleaned their accommodation, repainting some of it with green paint they had found, those not actually on guard could not be permitted to fester on their bunks, playing cards. Unoccupied soldiers get rusty quickly, his father had told him when he got his commission. An officer should see to it that they were always busy with tasks, otherwise there was trouble. There was no firing range – he had not been impressed by the battalion's marksmanship when he was first posted to it, though it had improved during their few weeks of training before the invasion of Holland – and they couldn't spend all their time rehearsing their already well-rehearsed weapons training. Nor could they play football or go for runs in boots and battle order all day. He rearranged the guard and patrolling rosters, then set his soldiers to clean paths throughout the park, sweeping them clear of leaves, cutting the border grass and repairing fencing. Soon, those parts of the park that the German Army maintained were gratifyingly tidier than the rest, which was looked after by the Kaiser's local Dutch gardeners. If they stayed here long enough, Krebbs thought, they could take over the running of the entire estate, improving it and saving the old man some money, too. Not that he needed more.

Krebbs had not spoken to the Kaiser since the dinner. The old man pottered about in the garden or among his ducks, usually in the mornings. He also made his regular stately progress from the house, across the lawns, through the rough grass and then through the oaks and beeches to his woodshed where his slow chopping or sawing could be heard for an hour or so. Sometimes there were estate workers stacking and preparing logs for him, sometimes only his dachshunds accompanied him.

Neither the Kaiser nor the Princess seemed interested, at that time, in exercising their right to leave the estate. They were not under arrest; Krebbs's orders were clear on that point. There were lunch and dinner parties for visiting friends – one exclusively Dutch but generally mixed German and Dutch – whose names and addresses had to be noted by the duty corporal, with Krebbs sending the list to HQ at the end of each week. So far as he could see, the invasion had made little difference to the Kaiser's social life; the Dutch still ate at his table. Krebbs also kept his own private log of sightings and events, in addition to his normal daily diary notes of his own times of rising, running and bathing. His diary was a black, leather-covered book which he had numbered fifteen, its predecessors being kept at home in Leipzig with his mother. It was a pleasure to think that in them was recorded for posterity every noteworthy event of his life from childhood onwards. Every external event, anyway; Krebbs had never sought to chart an interior life of whose importance he was unconvinced, and of whose very existence he was not sure he approved. You were what you did; the rest was froth. In one six-day period he noted nine sightings of Akki, referring to her as X and saying nothing else about her.

On the seventh morning a motorcycle despatch rider brought a signal from HQ SS in Holland. Marked 'Secret and Personal', it told him that, according to 'information received', the British government wished to persuade the Kaiser to defect to England, where his presence could be presented as a blow to the prestige and legitimacy of the Third Reich. They would exfiltrate him by secret means if he were willing, but it was thought possible they might consider abducting him if he were not. That would enable them to show the world that they could do as they pleased in German-occupied Europe. Winston Churchill, the British leader and principal war-monger, knew the Kaiser and had ordered that an invitation be secretly conveyed to him. It was understood that 'measures were already in train' to assess the Kaiser's attitude to such a proposal. This could mean that a trusted member of his entourage, or one of his regular visitors, was an English sympathiser.

Krebbs was therefore ordered to move with immediate effect into Huis Doorn itself and to ensure that the activities of the Kaiser's household were supervised and their attitudes observed and reported. He was to establish an armed physical presence in the house and to ensure that full identifying details of all visitors, as well as all other communications, were reported directly to HQ SS and not, as at present, forwarded from the Wehrmacht unit to which he was attached. He was not to reveal the real purpose of these changes but was to explain them by reference to the fact that the Luftwaffe fighter HQ was sited between Doorn and Utrecht and was believed to be a target for English saboteurs who might, if they were frustrated there, seek to murder the Kaiser.

The final paragraph complained that Krebbs's report on the Kaiser's attitude towards the Reich had still not been received at HQ SS, though it was known that the Wehrmacht had it. Finally – strictly for his information only – it was possible that a very senior leader might soon visit the Kaiser; details would follow in due course. Meanwhile, a sanitised version of this signal would be sent to Krebbs's Wehrmacht unit so that they were aware of the changes to be made and were reminded of the need to give Krebbs their fullest co-operation. If he experienced any problems he was to let HQ SS know at once.

Krebbs acknowledged the signal and immediately acted as instructed. After checking the correctness of his appearance, he marched across the park to the house to see von Islemann, the Kaiser's private secretary. It was eight-thirty in the morning, clear and bright, and the daily household prayers were just finishing in the vestibule. The Kaiser himself led the household in prayer and Krebbs listened from beyond the door to the rising and falling of his voice in practised modulation. Divorced from his words and from the Kaiser's habit of frequent heavy emphasis in conversation, it was a good voice, still – at his age – a fine and flexible instrument. People who had known him from his youth apparently described him as a natural artist who had never found his art. Listening to the prayers, with their incantations and murmured responses, reminded Krebbs of his own Catholic childhood. His mother and sister still went to mass but there had been few Catholics where they lived and as Krebbs grew up he increasingly disliked feeling different; he wanted to be like other people, so he left religion behind him.

After a scraping of chairs the doors opened and fifteen to twenty people came out. The household was larger than he had realised; more therefore to check on. A few left with the Kaiser through the door at the far end but most filed past Krebbs. They must have been surprised to see him, but they ignored him. Von Islemann and Akki came out simultaneously. He saw that she saw him but addressed himself immediately to von Islemann. They stood aside from the others. Their exchange was businesslike, correct and formal, not hostile but with no suggestion of ease or amiability. People shuffled past with faces averted, as in obvious demonstration that they were trying not to overhear. When Krebbs gave the authorised reason for the change, von Islemann nodded. Nothing seemed to surprise him.

'So, we are to be supervised for our own good, put under guard for our own protection?'

'That is correct.'

'And we must beware of English spies and saboteurs?'

The careful way von Islemann spoke made Krebbs feel he was being made fun of. His own speech became more officious. 'We must be watchful at all times, especially for English sympathisers.'

Von Islemann raised his eyebrows. 'Excluding, presumably, His Highness himself?'

Krebbs was installed in Huis Doorn by lunchtime. What he called his command post and what von Islemann called his office was the desk in the library corridor adjacent to the Kaiser's study and day-room. It had a telephone, monogrammed with the royal arms, and his position in the corridor meant that he could monitor access to the Kaiser. He could also observe the comings and goings of the staff, particularly the maids. Outside, on either side of the terrace in front of the house, the Dutch guard had built two semi-cellars, like unobtrusive blockhouses. Krebbs commandeered them to house whichever section he nominated for house duty. His platoon comprised three sections, which would mean one in and around the house with the other two based in the lodge, one on perimeter and grounds guard, the third resting or on fatigues. To prevent staleness, he would rotate them every few days. He was given a small room to himself in the basement, with a camp bed and just off the kitchen, a good, central point from which to cope with any trouble at night.

Later that morning the sky clouded over and it began to rain. The Kaiser put on his cape and fed his ducks on the moat, breaking the bread small and throwing it one piece at a time into the rain-dappled water. He did not go to his woodshed but spent the rest of the morning in his study, seated at his white, sloping desk with the adjustable saddle seat. He had one visitor, a Dutch doctor of horticultural science whom he evidently knew and who came to discuss the rosarium. Krebbs listened from outside the open door as they discussed the moving of more roses into the late Princess's garden. The Kaiser surprised Krebbs with his deep knowledge of flowers. The horticulturist remarked that there were now some 14,432 roses in the rosarium and in other parts of the estate. Krebbs noted the figure, along with details of the visitor and the exact time of his visit.

The many clocks made it a house of chimes, bells and tinkles. No two agreed precisely, and the ragged musical salvoes on the hour and half hour offended Krebbs's sense of order. While the clocks were variously announcing one o'clock, the Kaiser emerged from his study. Krebbs sprang to attention, as for a senior officer. He could not help himself.

The Kaiser had just lit a cigarette. There was humour in his watery blue eyes. 'So, now I have the privilege of a close guard?'

'Your Highness, the High Command –'

'The High Command is worried that I might be murdered by my Dutch hosts, who have tolerated my presence for over twenty years? Or bombed by the dastardly English in a last desperate throw before inevitable defeat? Or abducted on the orders of my second cousin, their king, perhaps? Or on the orders of my old acquaintance, Mr Winston Churchill, whom I knew as a pushy young man when most of the High Command were in their nappies?' He chuckled and puffed on his cigarette; the ash fell unregarded, the smoke coiled and expanded in the weak sunlight that now came through the window behind him. 'Very likely, very likely.'

He transferred his cigarette to his other hand and gripped Krebbs's shoulder, shaking him gently but irresistibly. 'Not that I object in any way, you understand. I am pleased that the High Command still thinks of me as of sufficient importance to merit close guard. And it is good that you are here; we shall have enjoyable conversations. You are properly accommodated, I trust? If you have any problems, speak to von Islemann. He is a good fellow even if, like me, he is incurably *ancien régime*.'

With his hand still on Krebbs's shoulder, they walked slowly downstairs to lunch. Krebbs felt almost as if he were under arrest. He stopped at the door. 'Your Highness, am I to join you for lunch?'

'Of course, dear boy, of course. You are part of the household now. Besides, how could you guard me if you did not? Suppose you had to explain to the High Command that I had been abducted over my soup?' He laughed and flicked ash into the air.

The Princess and von Islemann were already there. Neither betrayed any surprise at seeing Krebbs, for whom a servant discreetly laid an extra place while they stood by the window discussing the rosarium. It occurred to Krebbs that the Kaiser would make an easy target in the window for a sniper hidden on the perimeter of the park, or in the woods. He would have to think of such things now but, the trouble was, there was no end to them.

They sat down to a vegetable soup that looked ordinary enough but tasted better than anything Krebbs had had since mobilisation. The silver spoons and the imperial porcelain from which they ate seemed to emphasise the tastiness and he had to force himself not to eat too fast. The talk was still of roses.

Akki was one of the two maids who cleared the soup plates and served the fish to follow. He did not allow himself to look at her but when her arm reached over his shoulder for his bowl, his neck tingled. He had never been like this about a girl before. If he looked to his right he would meet the eye of the portly major-domo, overseeing the servants. If he looked to his left he would see Akki serving the Princess her fish. If he looked straight across, the Kaiser would think he was staring at him. He looked up instead, examining the portraits on the wall. There were two of the Kaiser, both minus his scar, and they were flanked by one of the late Princess and one of her successor. He was still aware of Akki's bowed head, with her straight centre parting and her tight bun, as she served von Islemann.

'If you are so engrossed by the picture, Herr Leutnant, what I wonder would you have to say to the original?' he heard the Princess say. Her plump wrinkled face smiled with disconcerting coquetry. It was as if she had put on a silly hat and now sought compliments.

'It is a very good likeness, your Highness,' he said.

'It does you less than justice, my sweet,' pronounced the Kaiser emphatically. 'I have always said so.'

'You flatter me, my dear. The Herr Leutnant is sadly all too correct. It is a faithful likeness of its all too rapidly fading subject.'

All except the servants turned to look up at the paintings. The major-domo whispered to Akki as she left the room.

'Nonsense, my dear,' said the Kaiser. 'But it must be admitted that those of me are better. I must be easier to capture – in oils, that is. Thanks to Untersturmführer Krebbs I am at this moment harder to capture in other ways. Eh?' He laughed. Everyone else smiled.

The Princess addressed Krebbs again, her lips still stretched in a smile. 'I hope we may capture an important guest soon. Someone who will be well known to you, I believe. I have been writing to friends and using my influence.'

'You must use influence sparingly, my dear,' said the Kaiser, 'and be careful with anything in writing. Sooner or later such things always come to light and may do harm. It is not wise to run after these Nazis too obviously. Their reich will not last a thousand years, whatever they say, and anyway if you chase them they will run away. Am I not right, eh?' He turned to von Islemann.

'One has to tread carefully with everyone nowadays,' said von Islemann.

The Princess's features became heavier and more fleshy.

She spoke quickly. 'Of course, of course, I realise that. I am always very careful where anything concerning Willie is concerned. But it is important to move things along where possible and if I can help, I shall. I wish to help. That is all.'

'My darling. I am sure you will be a very great help. It is simply that in anything connected with restoring me to my throne it is necessary to proceed with great caution, is it not?' The Kaiser looked again at von Islemann, who glanced at Krebbs.

'It is necessary at all times nowadays to exercise caution in everything,' said von Islemann.

Krebbs was discomforted to hear it asserted, casually, as if it were a mere matter of course, that the Third Reich would not last a thousand years. It was like talking about a person's forthcoming death in front of the person. It smacked of disloyalty. Even to have sat passively and heard it felt like a disloyal act.

The Kaiser fed himself with his right hand, using an implement that was knife and fork combined. He cut his fish into small pieces, scooped them up and pushed them into his mouth, chewing vigorously. 'God's ways are mysterious,' he said with his mouth full, turning to Krebbs. 'He makes me Kaiser, then He takes it away from me and sends me into exile, like Moses. He has His own reasons. Our duty is to accept them, not query them. But these Nazis – your people – are godless. They fear no gods. If He permits them to puff themselves up in this way, to have these great successes, and they truly are great successes' – he held up his fork as if it were a symbol – 'then it is my fear that He permits it in order to bring them down exceeding low, to make them as dust beneath His feet. And what will become of Germany in the process, eh? That is what worries me. It is the fate of Germany I grieve for, not that of any particular government. That is why we must help them to see clearly and judge wisely in these matters. We must talk quietly but we must not lecture.' He finished chewing and began cutting more fish.

No one said anything. Krebbs felt he was expected to respond but it was difficult for him to discuss the Party as if from outside. The benign tree whose shade had nurtured and sheltered him was not simply one of a number of trees he might have chosen; it was that which had given him life, almost. However, the Kaiser's reference to God offered him a way of responding that was neither confrontational nor compromising. If the Kaiser believed in God as his words suggested, then everything else obviously mattered less. Therefore, everything else he said mattered less. Therefore, Krebbs needed neither to challenge nor to accept it, but could say something neutral.

'German Christians must hope that God acts for the good of Germany,' he said, and was gratified to catch the tail of a swift, appraising glance from von Islemann.

'I am certain He does,' said the Princess.

'But one cannot have enough hatred for England,' the Kaiser said suddenly, his mouth again full. 'That is why I built my navy, to teach them a lesson. Yet at the same time' – he waved his fork – 'at the same time, it is to be remembered that I am myself half English. The good stubborn English blood that will not give way runs in my veins as in my mother's. They are not all bad, the English. But England just doesn't want to belong to Europe. For forty years I have been telling the world that England wants to form an independent part of the world between the continent and America or Asia. That cannot be permitted, especially as they are now in the grip of all these freemasons and Jews. Everything – everything we have must be turned into weapons in the fight against Anglo-American materialism and un-German behaviour. That is what I tried to do with our plays, our drama, when

I was first on the throne. If the Nazis can achieve this they will have done Germany and the world great service.'

Everyone nodded. The Princess smiled at Krebbs. 'As I said, we hope soon that our table will be graced by an important guest from the High Command.'

'And as for abducting me, no, the English would never do that,' the Kaiser continued. 'Other things, yes, they may try other things.'

'Assassination, do you mean?' asked the Princess.

The Kaiser laughed and made as if to cut his throat with his implement. 'No, no. It is true that their prime minister, Lloyd George, wanted me hanged after the last war but even he has changed his mind. Anyway, there must be others on their list before me – your Führer, for instance, Untersturmführer. But if they wish to assassinate people I would publicly advise them to concentrate on their true enemy, which is not the German people, not even the Nazis, but Juda. The Jews are like mosquitoes. They plague us all and are a nuisance that humanity must get rid of in some way or another. I have long said so. I believe the best would be gas, eh?' Still chewing, he touched his lips carefully with the corner of his napkin.

Krebbs and the Princess nodded again. Afterwards, at his desk upstairs, Krebbs made notes of the conversation. It was not easy, partly because he was unused to wine at lunchtime but also because it was hard to be both concise and comprehensive, as he had been taught that reports should be. It was all in his head, somewhere, but the act of sustained distillation on to the page felt like the mental equivalent of pull-ups in the gym. For some minutes he sat listening to the fifteen or sixteen clocks striking or chiming three, at times of their own choosing. The closest was in the corridor behind him, the next on the landing nearby. There were doubtless more than he could hear. As the last chime faded, the house was reoccupied by silence. The Kaiser was taking his afternoon nap in his day-room. Everything seemed to have closed down, apart from himself and the clocks. If he remained seated much longer, he felt, there would be only the clocks. He decided he would stretch his legs and keep himself awake by going round the house and synchronising them. He would use his officers' wristwatch, which was accurate to within thirteen seconds a week.

The first few clocks were straightforward; all were slow and had faces that opened easily. As with anything concerning accuracy, it was a satisfying task. He knew little of clocks, but enough to know that these were very fine, the best craftsmanship the old Germany could produce. His father, whose uncle had been a clockmaker, had known more about them and would have been delighted to handle such workmanship. As he edged the delicate hands forward, Krebbs felt he was trespassing upon them, although in a good cause. When he reached the grandfather clock in the yellow salon, however, he paused. It was fast by a full three minutes and he recalled his father saying that you should not, on such pendulum clocks, move the hands backwards. You had either to open the face and move the hands forwards by twenty-four hours minus three minutes, pausing on each hour to ensure that the chime remained synchronised, or you had to stop them until the correct time had caught up. There was something else you could do, something to do with removing the weight, if only he could remember. As it was, he could not even stop this clock because the case was locked and there was no sign of the key.

It was an elegant piece with an ornate head surrounded by nymphs and cupids. It narrowed to a neck before broadening into shoulders, from which the decorated case narrowed again to its feet. The tick of the pendulum was quiet but clear. Krebbs searched behind, beneath, on top for the key, then the mantelpiece, and finally the window-sill where he paused to look down at the moat. The sun had broken through again, glistening on the wet lilies and showing up the slow dark shapes of fish in the water. A blue dragon-fly floated up to the height of his window, then abruptly vanished. On the corner of the terrace one of his soldiers stood looking across towards the orangery, his rifle properly supported by its shoulder-strap. At the side, on the narrow wooden drawbridge that the Kaiser had built, stood Akki, looking down into the water. A few ducks loitered hopefully beneath the bridge.

She was bare-headed and wore a light grey short-sleeved dress. She stared into the water a few moments more, then crossed the bridge and walked slowly along the far side of the moat before turning across the grass towards the beeches and oaks some distance behind the house. She walked unhurriedly, as if going nowhere in particular. One of the dachshunds, Wei-wei, trotted across the bridge after her.

Krebbs caught up just as she entered the shade of the beeches. He had walked as fast as he could without, he hoped, appearing to his sentries to hurry. Not that that would stop them having a joke about it; no matter; he had her to himself. Anyway, he had legitimate official business with her.

She seemed unsurprised by his appearance, facing him as he approached and shading her eyes against the sunlight slanting through the leaves.

'May I join you?' he asked.

She indicated the wet hem of her dress. 'You are better prepared for a walk than I am, Untersturmführer. I had not realised how wet this long grass would be.'

It was not so much the careful precision of her German that struck him now but that she sounded so educated. She spoke with assurance. Wei-wei gave Krebbs a cursory bark and resumed his snuffling beneath some brambles.

'I saw you on the bridge, looking into the water as if you had dropped something.'

She turned back to the path through the trees. 'I was thinking.'

'May I ask what your thoughts were?'

'Not yet.'

'I may ask later, then?'

'Perhaps.'

He hoped her thoughts might be about him. 'But I must ask you another question, an official question. I am required to ask you the date of your arrival here and your address in your home town and the full names of your parents.'

'Why?' She seemed amused.

'It is occupation regulations.'

'For everyone?'

'Yes, but for everyone here especially. It is for the protection of His Highness.'

'From what?'

It was absolutely against regulations to divulge such information to those who did not need to know but he wanted her to see that he was important enough to possess it. 'I cannot tell you. Let us say, from disaffected elements.'

They were approaching a bench by a pond. 'Do you have your officer's special notebook and pencil?'

'Of course.'

They sat. She answered his questions calmly and he made his notes carefully, in his best script. Her voice sounded as if she were quietly mocking, trying not to laugh, but whenever he looked up she was serious. His knee was very close to hers, not quite touching. When they had finished he left his notebook on his lap and leaned back, stretching his arm along the top of the bench behind her and edging his knee a fraction closer. 'His Highness himself has a curious attitude towards his cousins, our

68

English enemy. He says he hates them but at the same time he seems to admire and feel part of them.'

She leaned back, looking into the pond. She must, he thought, be aware of how close she was to his arm. 'He is,' she said. 'He says that in Germany he was never trusted because of his English sympathies and English mother and that in England he was never trusted because he was German and made bellicose statements. He is probably happiest here, in Holland. It is the only permanent home he has ever had.'

He moved his arm so that his fingers and the edge of his wrist just touched her shoulder. They both stared at the pond. He feared that if he moved closer she would feel his heart pounding. 'Is he happy that the German Army is here now, do you think?'

'I don't know. He accepts it, certainly, as he accepts most things now.'

'You sound as if you have studied His Highness's history.'

He spoke jokingly but she turned to him seriously. 'He talks to me sometimes, that is all. He is lonely.'

She remained facing him, very close. He kissed her on the lips. She was passive but unresisting. He prolonged the kiss, holding her shoulder and pulling her to him, his other hand on her knee. She smelt of some perfume, or soap, something nice anyway that he had not smelt for a long time, and she was soft and warm. The problem, he was thinking behind his closed eyes, was what to do next, when the kiss stopped; how to move to the next stage, if there were to be one. He wondered, too, why she was letting him do it, but did not want to break momentum by asking.

It was she who broke off and moved back a little. 'Herr Offizier, your gun is uncomfortable.'

His holster was squashed between them. He shifted it

creakingly on his belt. Her head was still turned away but she remained leaning against his arm. 'And we were discussing His Highness, I think,' she continued.

'Of course, yes, for a moment I was forgetting about His Highness. I cannot think why.' He traced the line of her eyebrow with the tip of his middle finger. 'He is a confused man, clearly, but at least he is sound on the Jewish question.' She looked thoughtful in repose, with an inwardness he yearned to plumb. She was twenty-nine, he knew now from his questions, six years older than himself, more mature than the girls he was used to. An older woman, more experienced than himself. Perhaps she was using him in some way; he didn't mind, it was exciting. 'His mind is not divided on that subject, at least. He would kill them all.'

'He wouldn't kill anyone. He is all words. He is really quite soft.' She stood and walked to the pond.

'You are fond of him? You like him?'

'He is a complicated man who does not know himself.' She turned and continued along the path through the trees without waiting for him.

He had no sooner caught up than he realised they were no longer alone. Their path curved gradually back towards the house and was joined on the way by another, along which some woodsmen, carrying saws and axes, were walking. Their voices echoed through the trees. 'Akki,' he said, keeping close and speaking quietly, 'is it possible that we may meet again?'

'Is it possible that we shall not?'

'I mean alone, so that we can talk. I should like to talk more to you.'

'Would you, Martin? Really?'

It was thrilling, quite ridiculously thrilling, to hear her use his name. It made him feel they were closer, despite her still slightly mocking tone.

'I should like to talk and talk and talk. May we meet again like this?'

'If you wish.'

The woodsmen were nearer now. 'I shall arrange it,' he said.

For the rest of that day Krebbs felt full of energy. When he wrote up the staff details the mere transcription of her name gave him secret pleasure. He was unexpectedly successful in securing a motorcycle despatch rider from headquarters to pick up his signal that same afternoon, and he got the man to take back his soldiers' letters home instead of waiting for the next post pick-up. He reorganised the guard rosters and got up a scratch game of five-a-side football for those not on duty. He played himself, in goal. Afterwards, he took a few volunteers for a long run. He felt he could take pride in his new platoon now. They had shaken down together and got used to him, even though he was an attached officer. They were fit, eager, lively, jokey among themselves, almost as wolfishly ready for action as his own SS platoon had been when they moved into Belgium and France. They didn't quite have the edge of Waffen SS troopers, of course, not those few final percentage points of missionary zeal, but their improvement in the past week or two was evident from their bearing, their fully-alive eyes, their promptness and turnout. He was struck again by the seeming paradox that soldiers were at their best in the business of death – their own or their enemy's – when themselves most vividly alive. His chief worry now was that they would go off. Whatever efforts he made to enliven and vary their routine, long periods of static duty were not good for soldiers. He wanted to lead them into battle and then return to Doorn. Between bouts of focus and concentration, he daydreamed of their being sent off to some fighting like that they had had around Dunkirk and of his then returning, battle-scarred

71

but triumphant, to Akki. Only this time a proper, textbook battle with no unexpected rehearsals and no unpalatable aftermath.

The Kaiser was writing in his study when Krebbs returned to his desk in the early evening. Seen from the door, he was largely backside, leaning forward on his saddle seat to write at his white sloping desk, a cigarette smouldering in his ashtray. Later, Krebbs heard him wheezing and sighing as he dismounted; next he heard the shuffling of books on shelves, then the creaking of an armchair and more exhaling. It was odd that the old, who had less breath, should breathe so much more loudly than the young. Krebbs felt supple and relaxed after his exertions that afternoon. It was not good, he felt, for the young to be around the elderly for too long. Age might be contagious.

'Are you there, Untersturmführer?'

Krebbs went in. The Kaiser sat with a book open on his lap, a fresh cigarette between his nicotined fingers. 'Do you read?' he asked, without looking round.

'Yes, your Highness.'

'I mean, do you read books – novels?'

Krebbs could not recall the last novel he had read. It must have been in his childhood. He preferred real things to novels, though he liked films.

'You should,' continued the Kaiser, without waiting for a reply. 'They tell you about life. Not just about what happens, which is what history tells you, but about life itself. They make you see it. We have some very fine German novelists, even some of those who have deserted Germany now like that man Feuchtwanger who wrote *Jew Süss*. Do you remember that? Probably you are too young, but it was also a film. You can learn all you want about power and Jewishness from that book, more than from any history. Whatever else one may say about them, they are remarkable people, remarkable.'

'The Jews, your Highness?'

The Kaiser raised his white eyebrows. 'Who else? Feuchtwanger is one himself, of course, and a communist, which is the worst combination possible, but his book precisely captures the ambivalence of being Jewish. Only the Jews can write so well about their own bad qualities. When I was young I had a close friend, Siegfried Sommer, who was Jewish. Now, because of this book, I see there was the same thing in him. Then, he was just my friend.'

Krebbs was unsure what to say. 'He changed, sire?'

'Changed? I don't know about that. He was what he always was, only of course I did not see it all. But I prefer Wodehouse, really. Do you know Wodehouse? An English author. He is even better than this Jewish man. Very funny. I shall read you something of his one day.'

He turned back to his book and continued reading and smoking as if Krebbs were no longer there. After a few moments Krebbs quietly left the room. At his desk he took out his pocket book and began summarising what the Kaiser had said, but before he finished he subsided once again into his own daydreams.

FIVE

While Krebbs was still shaving the following morning he was summoned to the field telephone he had had installed in the brick passage outside his room. The gatehouse guard reported a despatch rider with an urgent signal marked personal for Krebbs: should they send him up or would Krebbs come down to the gatehouse? He ordered them to send the man up and cut himself on the right cheek in his hurry to finish.

The signal was from HQ SS, in the name of Hans Rauter, the lieutenant-general in charge of all SS operations in Holland. It informed him that the head of Schutzstaffel, Reichsführer SS Heinrich Himmler, was to visit Prince Wilhelm that day, and would stay the night. The principle of such a visit had been arranged through the Princess's contacts in Berlin, but for security reasons neither she nor Prince Wilhelm knew when it was to take place. The short notice was deliberate, also in the interests of security. Krebbs was to inform them and to arrange for the accommodation of the Reichsführer and his staff in the house. Neither the Prince's staff nor the Wehrmacht guard were to be told the visitor's identity in advance. Krebbs was to conduct a thorough security search of the house before arrival and to ban all visitors from house and grounds throughout the stay.

He hurried upstairs to his desk to check whether he had notes of any visitors due that day. He had not, but that did not mean there would not be any. Without access to the Kaiser's and the Princess's diaries, which were kept by von Islemann, he could not be sure. He remained standing by his desk, deliberately calming himself. The thought of dealing with the Reichsführer was unsettling. This man was second only to the Führer, the purest of the pure, creator of the SS, feared by some even more than Hitler, feared even by the other leaders. The Ignatius Loyola of the Party, Hitler had called him. Like Krebbs, he had been born a Catholic.

Krebbs had never met him, of course, though Himmler had taken the salute at the SS Junkerschule passing-out parade. Now he would deal with him in person, with almost no time to prepare. He remained standing by the desk, his stomach fluttering and the muscles in his legs quivering, as though he had just run hard and was about to run again. It was like before going into battle, waiting to cross the start line. Yet the man was a mere mortal like himself; if you cut him he'd bleed. Or if a shell landed next to him, as had happened to Krebbs's company commander in France, he would dissolve in a mere shower of blood. Yet still Krebbs trembled.

There was, in fact, nothing to do yet. The guard had to have their breakfast, as he should his own. The household – the principals, at least – had not yet stirred, though there was activity in the kitchen. The grandfather clock behind him struck six-thirty, already a little ahead of the others despite his attentions. Outside the dew sparkled on the lawns and the sun glinted on the moat. A beautiful day that would pass, like other days, come what may. Whoever we were, we all had to live through days, one after another

76

after another. They were the condition and measure of our lives, even the greatest and most exotic of lives, such as that of Reichsführer SS Heinrich Himmler.

To have the security of the Reichsführer in his care, however briefly, was an honour. His father would have been proud; his mother would not know what to think when he told her – if he was permitted. Akki, too, would surely be impressed. And the Wehrmacht adjutant back at battalion HQ would have to sit up and take notice. But it was necessary to get it right. As soon as he had told the Kaiser and the Princess he would personally search and inspect every room of the house, partly for security and partly to help him decide whom should be billeted where. The Reichsführer, of course, would have the Hessian suite formerly occupied by the Kaiser's brother, Prince Henry, once a frequent visitor. He would check that first, then go up to the servants' rooms in the attic, and work systematically downwards. He would have to check Akki's room, a good thing for other reasons. It was important to know whether she shared a room, or had her own.

The Kaiser and the Princess breakfasted in the small dining-room. When Krebbs entered the Princess was sitting back in her chair, talking about someone and fiddling with her napkin, alternately crunching it and pulling it apart. The Kaiser sat over his coffee, lighting his first cigarette of the day with a lighter shaped like a small silver cannon. Von Islemann was eating with them, which surprised Krebbs. Von Islemann was staff and therefore not permitted to know that the Reichsführer was coming.

The Princess smiled and bade Krebbs good morning. The Kaiser simply stared as he exhaled, saying nothing. Von Islemann nodded and sipped his coffee. Krebbs remained by the door, standing at attention as befitted the news he had. He chose his words carefully. 'Your Highness, your guest from Berlin arrives today. He will stay tonight. I must inspect the house, if you please. Meanwhile, it is requested that the staff are not informed of your guest's identity in advance.' He summarised the rest of the signal.

The Princess threw her napkin theatrically into the air, letting it fall to the floor behind her. 'This is wonderful news. Something happens at last. You see, Willie, it is as I told you: you have to make the first move with these people because they do not know how to approach you. They are too much in awe. Now with Himmler coming, it is almost as good as Hitler. It shows they are serious. We must show that we appreciate that. We shall use the Großen table service.'

The Kaiser shook his head. 'The Neuosier service, my dear. That is the imperial service I had made, that was made for me, in the Berlin porcelain manufactory. It would be more appropriate and it is more replaceable than the Großen. One does not know how these people behave at table.'

The Princess laughed. 'Really, Willie, I am sure Herr Himmler knows how to hold his knife and fork. Indeed, he has royal connections, has he not, with Prince Heinrich of Bavaria?'

'More like a railway connection than anything royal. His father was tutor to the princeling who later became young Himmler's godfather and after whom the boy was named Heinrich. Von Islemann is more royal than that, probably also Untersturmführer Krebbs for all we know, eh?' The Kaiser waved his cigarette and laughed.

'Forgive me, your Highness, but my orders are that the staff are not permitted to know the identity of the visitor in advance,' repeated Krebbs, looking at von Islemann. He felt awkward but it was essential to be correct.

The Kaiser appeared not to have heard him. 'Surely, your aunts were more royal?' he asked von Islemann. 'The four that were starved by the English, eh? How many aunts did you have?'

'Seven, your Highness.'

'Seven?' The Kaiser pulled at his cigarette. 'That is enough aunts, I think. A sufficiency of aunts.' He laughed again, his left hand resting on his belly.

The Princess looked at Krebbs, not unkindly. 'Von Islemann is entirely trustworthy. You need not worry about him, Herr Leutnant. He is more than staff, almost family. He will help you in your preparations.'

Von Islemann smiled slightly and nodded at Krebbs as though they were fellow conspirators. 'The Untersturm-führer is of course correct to follow his instructions precisely, but I am sure that his superiors would at the same time wish him to interpret them in such a way that they be most effectively fulfilled.' Afterwards, he followed Krebbs up to his desk in the corridor. 'No doubt you have everything under proper control, Untersturmführer, but please say if there is anything you need. The household staff are well accustomed to receiving important guests and you may be sure they will do everything properly. But there is always the unexpected and I know well what anxiety such visits can cause. Please regard me as being at your disposal.'

Although von Islemann spoke no less formally than ever, this time Krebbs did not detect any mocking or patronising edge. He stood and nodded his acknowledgement. 'Thank you, Herr Hauptmann. I shall not hesitate to ask if need be.'

'Does your guest stay long?'

'One night only, I am informed.'

'A pity. It would be instructive to see more of him. Although perhaps we shall find that one evening's conversation is sufficient to form an accurate impression.' His slight, complicitous, smile returned. 'Good luck, Untersturmführer.'

Apart from the household arrangements, Krebbs had also to ensure that the guard was spick and span, that the gatehouse was smart and those on duty briefed. Unfortunately, there was no time to cut the lawns. It was not for his soldiers to do, of course, but they would have made a better job of it than the slow-moving Dutch gardeners. He got them sweeping the paths again, which improved things. Two were due for leave that day, but he cancelled that.

It was nearly mid-morning by the time he reached the servants' rooms in the attic. They were small and without fireplaces but at least they were individual, so there was some privacy despite the flimsy wooden walls. Only in coming or going was there a chance of being observed, unless, between you, you made too much noise. There were no locks on the doors.

He had not seen Akki that morning and she was not in her room. It was her morning off, one of the other girls said. She had gone into the village but would be back before lunch. She hadn't, of course, known about any important visitors when she left.

Krebbs contemplated the chaste single bed, her clothes and uniform on the hook behind the door – there was no wardrobe, no room for one – and the plain kitchen chair bearing a cheap red alarm clock and a Dutch novel. On the small chest of drawers were a washbasin and jug, her hairbrush and other small bits and pieces, with a mirror propped against the wall. A low, open door led into an eaves cupboard, in which he could see an old brown suitcase flat on the floor with a pair of black shoes on top. Also on the chair by the bed was a tiny vase of flowers he couldn't identify but which gave off a faint scent. Like the other servants' rooms, it was impersonal and temporary, yet the modesty of her possessions compared with the clutter of her colleagues and her economical orderliness

– with the exception of the open eaves cupboard – made it seem paradoxically more personal. He was alone, and could have opened all the drawers and searched everything, as he had the others, but didn't. All he did was pick up the book. It looked like a love-story, with a picture of a dark-haired girl on the cover wearing a red blouse and a black skirt. She looked a little like Akki herself, though her hair was shorter and more wavy. He opened the book at the page with the bookmark, saw it was all dense text and no dialogue, and put it down.

Later, the Princess summoned him. She was in the Yellow Room, her own sitting-room, alone but for an audience of painted Hohenzollerns. Since breakfast she had changed into more formal clothes, a green dress with long buttoned sleeves and small lace cuffs. She again wore her long pearl necklace and pendant pearl earrings. Rouge made her puffy cheeks look bigger.

'Herr Leutnant,' she began, the moment Krebbs appeared, 'we have a task to perform together. Between us, we have to ensure that this visit is a success for all concerned. It is my devout hope that Herr Himmler is coming to invite Willie – His Majesty – to return and take up the throne again, to be titular head of the German people in their time of need and danger. This is what I have been working for, through my contacts.' She played with a lace handkerchief in her large hands, as she had the napkin at table. 'It is what Willie hopes for, too, I know, but because he hopes for it so very much he cannot bring himself to admit it for fear of disappointment and that is why he speaks as he did earlier about Herr Himmler and the Nazis. Really, he admires them and would love to be back in Berlin with them, helping them in their struggle. But he fears rejection. If he were rejected a second time it would surely kill him. I hope he will be sensible with Herr Himmler, with whom I am sure he will find much in common' – she

81

smiled anxiously, twisting her handkerchief – 'but I hope too that you understand his predicament and if necessary can explain to Herr Himmler the background. I hope I can myself but it is not always easy if one is a member of the royal family, and you must know Herr Himmler and know better how to talk to him. And if you have any worries, if you are thinking any misunderstandings are developing, you will please, please tell me so that together we may prevent them?'

It was novel for Krebbs to be given a sense of political power, however exaggerated her conception of his influence. 'Of course, your Highness, I shall be happy to help in any way I can.'

She looked almost tearfully relieved. Her eyes shone and she clenched her handkerchief. 'Thank you, thank you. And you – you have family, yes?' She nodded as he told her, smiling all the time. 'I should like to help them somehow. Perhaps we may discuss it after the visit.'

Krebbs was puzzled for a moment, then embarrassed, but there was no time to linger. 'Of course, your Highness.'

Later, while Krebbs was telephoning the gatehouse from his desk, the Kaiser came out of his study, puffing a small cigar and holding another book, which he pushed between Krebbs's face and the phone. 'The English author, remember? Wodehouse. The one you should read.'

Although irritated by the old man's regal – or perhaps child-like – assumption of priority, his constant failure to acknowledge or even notice what anyone else was doing, Krebbs put down the phone. The book was in English.

'There, you see?' continued the Kaiser. 'Very funny, eh? English humour. Mine too, though of course I also have German humour.' He laughed and blew smoke into Krebbs's face.

'I don't read English, your Highness.'

'You don't? You don't?' The Kaiser raised his eyebrows in mock surprise. 'I shall translate it for you later.' He stood reading to himself for a while, smiling and nodding, before walking slowly back into his study.

Krebbs picked up the phone again. The gatehouse had been in the middle of saying something about visitors. As he waited for them to answer he saw Akki walking back across the park, carrying a black shopping bag. Again, she paused as she crossed the moat. There would be no time to see her that day. He was sharp with the gatehouse when they answered.

Later, when he was in the kitchen in the midst of an unsatisfactory discussion about catering, he was summoned again by the Kaiser and Princess. They were in the Gobelin Room, he was told, as if he would know which that was. It turned out to be the reception hall, named after the ancient tapestries hanging from the walls. Husband and wife stood in silence when he entered, each facing a different window. The Kaiser held a fresh cigarette in his right hand. He turned as soon as Krebbs entered. His face looked heavier and darker.

'So, I am a prisoner in my own house? And my friends are not permitted to visit me? And I presumably am not allowed to leave if I wish? This is your doing, Untersturmführer, you and your wonderful Schutzstaffel. May I beg – may His Majesty the Kaiser beg' – he affected a mocking bow – 'an explanation, eh?'

The Princess stepped forward. 'Willie, please, this is not –'

'Thank you, my dear, I am quite sure our wonderful Schutzstaffel, our wonderful protection squad, which is here to protect us, is quite capable of answering for itself.'

The Princess's fleshy features were riven with concern. 'Willie – His Highness – was disturbed to receive a telephone call from Herr and Frau Schwarz, friends of ours who had called to see us and were turned away by your soldiers at the gatehouse, with no explanation. They feared that something terrible had happened, perhaps even that we had been taken away.' Her voice tailed off and she stared at Krebbs in anxious appeal.

Remaining at attention always gave Krebbs confidence because it was so obviously correct; it could not be faulted. He addressed the Kaiser formally. 'As your Highness may recall from my description of the signal I received, all visitors to Huis Doorn and the grounds were forbidden from the time I received the signal until after the Reichsführer's visit. This is for the security of the Reichsführer and also for your Highness's, since if his presence here were known Doorn might be attacked by disaffected elements or by English aircraft. My soldiers have orders to explain to visitors that this is a temporary measure and to take names and addresses so that your Highness may contact them afterwards and give a suitable explanation. I regret it if this has not occurred and shall make inquiries. Meanwhile, I offer my apologies. But the exclusion of visitors must continue.'

Taking pleasure in his own correctness, Krebbs continued looking the Kaiser directly in the eye after he had finished. His was now the voice of power, of real, present, palpable power. The Kaiser must know that as well as anyone.

The Kaiser said nothing for a few moments. Blue smoke still rose in a thin line from his cigarette as he stared back at Krebbs. When eventually he spoke his voice was quiet. 'The time was when no one said no to the Kaiser in such a way. The Kaiser saw whom he chose when he chose. Other people knew their places and other organisations were not too mighty. But God saw to it that the Kaiser fell, so that he became as nothing. In just this way will He bring down others, be they never so mighty.'

He put his cigarette to his lips and walked slowly from the room.

The Princess waited until his footfalls had faded, then smiled weakly. She was almost in tears. 'Poor Willie, he takes it so badly. It is always a sign that he is upset when he mentions God. He cannot bring himself to ask for anything from this new Reich. They must ask him. It is not because he doesn't like them, it's because of what he was, what he still is. I do hope they will see that.' Her finger traced the marquetry on one of the chests of drawers. The action appeared to revive her. 'Does Herr Himmler bring Margarete, his wife, with him?'

'The signal says his wife is ill and remains in Berlin. He will bring two adjutants and his secretary, Hedwig Potthast.'

The Princess inspected her fingertip for dust. 'Of course, Fräulein Mouse. It will not be necessary for you to find them separate rooms, I think.'

A second signal gave the Reichsführer's estimated time of arrival as four p.m. That relaxed things a little, particularly with the kitchen since there was no need to worry about lunch. The Princess had said that she and the major-domo would decide the dinner menu. Having therefore made all the arrangements he could, Krebbs was free to re-inspect, he explained to the corporal of the guard, those parts of the house he had searched only superficially.

Akki was in her room. Her grey eyes showed something apart from surprise when she answered his knock. It gratified him to have an effect.

'I'm glad it's you,' she said, smiling after a moment. 'At first when I saw your uniform I thought you were Herr Himmler himself.'

'Herr Himmler?'

'He is the visitor, is he not? The one who is coming

today? He is the reason I have to return to duty on my morning off.'

'You should not have been told his identity. Who told you?'

'Nobody told us. Nobody tells us anything, so we have to find out everything for ourselves. The Kaiser and the Princess were overheard talking, that is all. What does it matter? We shall know anyway when he comes.' She wore the checked, short-sleeved, v-necked dress he had seen her in earlier, the alternative maids' dress to the longer black ones they sometimes wore. It ended just below the knee, showing most of her calves. As she spoke she looped a clean white apron over her head. Her eyes were playful. 'You look so serious when you think something is wrong.'

'I have come to inspect your room, as I have inspected all the others. I was here before when you were out but I preferred to inspect it with you.'

'I hope you will find everything correct, Untersturm-führer.'

'It is very tidy and so far I have found no saboteurs. The eaves cupboard door was open before but now it is closed, so it is even tidier.'

She glanced at the cupboard as she reached behind her waist to tie the apron, pulling it tight across her. He went over to the bed and picked up the book from the chair. 'What is this?'

'A book.'

'What kind of book, please?'

'Not a book for soldiers. Still less for Schutzstaffel.'

Afterwards, he could never precisely recollect the sequence, though he tried often. She was standing very close to him and at some point must have relieved him of the book, though whether his arm was already around her or whether he put it around her as she did it, he could not say. It was even possible that he had put the book down himself. The next he knew they were kissing, properly and fully this time, and he was crushing her to him. She seemed to take possession of him, as he of her, making him feel at once helpless and invigorated. They subsided clumsily on to the bed, his boot knocking the chair.

She stopped him. 'Not now, please. Not now.'

'There's time. It's all right. We've got time. No one will bother us here.' His voice sounded thicker to his own ears.

'They will, I'm due downstairs now.' She tried to wriggle out from under him. 'Someone will come up. It would not be good for my position here. Nor for yours.'

He grinned, lying on top of her and pinning her arms to the pillow. Their faces were still very close, almost touching. 'My position feels very good just now. So does yours.'

'Von Islemann would find out. He would tell the Princess. And then Herr Himmler would find out and that would be bad for you.'

'Why should Herr Himmler mind? He has his mistress and is bringing her with him.'

'But she is not Jewish.'

Krebbs said nothing. After a while he rolled over, and let her get up. She went to the mirror on the chest of drawers, straightened her hair and re-tied her apron. Krebbs remained on the bed, resting on his elbow.

'Why did you tell me?'

'I thought you would wish to know. I wanted you to.'

'Why?'

'Because I like you.'

'Why do you think it is important for me to know this fact?'

'It might make a difference for you.'

She did not look round. He watched her face as she reordered her hair in the mirror but she did not meet his eyes. He got up and stood behind her. 'Why do you think it might make a difference?'

'Does it not? It must do, surely. It does to many people here in Holland. It must do even more to you Germans. It does to me, too.'

She removed her hair-slide and held it between her teeth while repositioning her bun. He wanted her even more now than before.

'Don't worry, you won't have caught anything, it's not contagious.' She fastened the clip.

'I wasn't thinking that.'

'It's what you believe, isn't it? You people in Shutzstaffel? Contact with us would corrupt and besmirch you.'

'Have you told anyone else here? Does anyone else know?'

'Only you.'

'It is dangerous to tell people. Even with me, you are taking a risk. Especially with me, many would say. Why did you take such a risk?'

'I told you.'

It was curious that he should want her even more now. Curious, too, that already he should feel he was betraying something. He had not actually done anything, yet he knew that that was not what was important. Could all he had been told and believed about contact with Jews, especially their filthy women, evaporate so easily, after a few conversations and a couple of minutes on the bed? And with a housemaid? That he could let everyone down so easily, so comprehensively, was shocking. But, now that it had happened, it seemed unsurprising, felt almost normal. Of course there must be Jews and Jews. Some Jews were less Jewish than others, perhaps.

'I must go.' She turned and faced him.

'Do you dislike me for being a German soldier?'

'I don't like what you represent but I like you for being Martin. That's why I told you. I wanted you to know.'

'How can you say that when you hardly know me?' She stood with her arms folded. He put his hands on her shoulders. 'I don't mind that you are Jewish. Really. It's all right with me.' Saying it made him feel it could become true.

'It's not all right *for* you, Martin.'

'It is if I think it is.'

'It's not what you think that matters, is it? Not if you are to be a loyal soldier of the Reich. You are not supposed to think. The trouble is, Martin, I sense you are a decent boy – man – at some level you do not even know yourself. You are nicer than you want to be. That is why I like you. That is also why contact with me is bad for you. It could harm you.' She looked away from him. 'Now, I must go, please.'

'May I come to you later?'

'If you want.'

He moved aside and she slipped out of the room without looking back.

The Reichsführer was on time. At a minute to four the gatehouse rang and Krebbs had barely put down the phone when he saw the green, open-topped BMW sweeping along the drive, followed by another, closed, car. The headlights of the BMW were blacked out but its famous black-on-white number, SS-1 – the letters rendered as lightning flashes – was clearly visible. Inside were four figures in the black caps of SS full dress uniform, their silver insignia picked out by the afternoon sun. It was always a thrill to see the full SS uniform, lifting everything suddenly to a new tempo. Krebbs took up his own cap, settled it exactly in the gilded mirror on the landing, and hurried downstairs. By the time the car drew up on the gravel he was at the foot of the steps, his Heil Hitler salute as rigid as one of the lightning flashes. The guard presented arms smartly.

The Reichsführer was instantly recognisable by his gold pince-nez and his trim moustache. Unusually for a VIP, he sat in the front and got out without waiting for the door to be opened. He returned Krebbs's salute, saying 'Heil Hitler!' in a quiet, precise voice, then smiled. 'Untersturmführer Krebbs?' he asked pleasantly.

'Yes, sir. Good afternoon, sir.'

'Thank you for making these arrangements at such short notice. You have an important task here. We must talk later. Please lead on.'

They mounted the steps with his adjutants, who introduced themselves as Obersturmbannführer Grothman and Sturmbannführer Macher. Two or three other men and a woman got out of the second car. Krebbs had arranged that they should be escorted by his senior corporal, while his soldiers took care of the luggage. He mounted the steps alongside but slightly behind the Reichsführer. Himmler was plumper and shorter than he had anticipated, short enough to make Krebbs feel awkward when near him. The adjutants, both taller, walked in step behind.

Krebbs could see Princess Hermine, in her green dress, waiting just inside the door. For a moment he feared she was alone, the Kaiser having refused to greet his guest, but then the portly figure appeared beside her, wearing his field grey uniform. That was a good sign, thought Krebbs, an astute choice, nothing too grand but suggestive of comradeship, identity and shared purpose.

The introductions went easily. The Reichsführer continued smiling pleasantly and addressed his hosts as prince and princess, his manner respectful but not obsequious. The adjutants saluted and clicked heels impeccably. The rest of the party, an NCO, two troopers and Hedwig

Potthast, joined them. Fräulein Potthast was introduced, bobbing a neat curtsey. She had short brown hair and wore a brown jacket and skirt, with a cream blouse. She was no beauty but a quiet, restful sort of woman, Krebbs thought.

The Kaiser's manner was formal. He did not lead on into the house but remained still after the introductions, compelling everyone else to do the same. There was a pause that threatened to become awkward until it became apparent that the Kaiser was waiting to make a speech. He faced his guests with his left hand clasped before him in his right. 'We are honoured that the Reichsführer, without doubt one of the busiest men in Germany during these pressing times, should visit us in our humble retirement abode,' he said, addressing Himmler. 'Here, in our exile, we have been forced to support the Reich's great project from afar, but now, in these new circumstances, we hope we may be able to use our influence, such as it is, to make a more positive contribution to the great cause. Germany has renewed and reinvigorated itself, a model for the rest of the world. A new Germany was needed, and forth she sprang. Now, a new world order is needed and it is for the new Germany to lead the way. The Reichsführer, who honours us with his presence today, has been a beacon to the new Germany. We pray that he may be a beacon also to the new world that is to follow. If we can add our moiety to help, we shall count it more than a great privilege: it will make our life complete.'

Led by the adjutants, everyone clapped. Himmler stepped forward, clasping his hands before him as the Kaiser had. The sun coming through the open door caught one side of his face, making it look unwholesomely pale and his shapely, rather feminine lips, colourless and thin. In profile, his chin receded almost seamlessly into flaccid and wrinkled skin. His cap, with its prominent Death's

Head badge, looked suddenly too big for him. Krebbs was unwillingly reminded of a boy in man's uniform.

'On behalf of our revered Führer and of the leaders of the Reich and of the people of Germany, I present compliments to Prince Wilhelm and Princess Hermine and express our relief and joy that the German nation and its Prince should be reunited at last. Our mission to unite the whole of Europe in an ever-closer union and to restore to it its sense of destiny and purpose will indeed, we trust, prove a beacon to the world so that together we can cleanse ourselves of all those influences that have harmed and hindered humanity for so long.' His quietness was reassuring, his emphases carefully modulated as though he were a doctor expounding a certain cure to intelligent laymen. 'We further hope – dare to hope – that the Prince and Princess may contribute to Germany's international mission, in which the persuasion of other powers of the rightness and justice of our purpose, and of our common cause with them in bringing about a world of moral order, equality and prosperity, will be crucial to the success and continuance of the Reich. Heil Hitler!'

Led by Himmler, heels clicked and arms shot upwards. For Krebbs it was so automatic that he was never conscious of the decision to do it. The Princess half raised her arm as in hesitant greeting. The Kaiser kept his hands clasped but nodded to the Reichsführer.

Prince Henry's former quarters were in the tower at the rear of the house, and included an octagonal room. As the Princess had predicted, it was taken for granted that Fräulein Potthast would share it with the Reichsführer. While the house servants brought in their luggage, she wandered unhurriedly about the rooms, examining everything. Himmler threw his cap on the bed. His brown hair, short at the back and sides, was pressed smooth and brushed back on top. He loosened his belt, looking about as if he had just arrived on holiday. Krebbs made to withdraw.

'One moment, Untersturmführer, if you please.' The Reichsführer nodded at the servants and waited until they had closed the door behind them. 'Please take off your cap and stand easy. I want to ask you some questions while we are alone on subjects on which I should value your opinion.'

He sat at the desk, side on, and indicated that Krebbs should take one of the other hard-backed chairs. Fräulein Potthast, having finished her inspection, continued the unpacking of their bags that the servants had begun. Her presence evidently did not compromise the idea that they were alone. Himmler folded his hands on his lap. His grey-blue eyes gazed through his pince-nez with an air of peaceful interrogation. 'You have been here long enough to observe the former Kaiser, Prince Wilhelm, and his household. Your reports were forwarded to me and I read them with interest. I read many reports in the course of my duties and I am happy to say that yours compare favourably with the great majority. They are correctly written and pertinent. There were one or two areas of particular interest and it is these I now wish to address.'

Krebbs did not know how to respond to praise. He feared he might blush with pleasure. He felt awkward enough, anyway, sitting in the presence of the Reichsführer, holding his cap in his lap and trying not to sit too rigidly. At the same time, it was important not to appear too relaxed; the Reichsführer's bureaucratic formulations and circumlocutions, delivered in his quiet, even tones, were slightly hypnotic.

'Firstly, I should be interested to know more of Prince Wilhelm's true attitudes towards the Reich. He seems, according to your reports and other information in our possession, in this as in some other areas, to be ambiguous, even self-contradictory. Could you describe in a few sentences what you believe to be his true feelings?'

Krebbs tried not to clutch his cap too hard. 'I believe, sir, that he admires the Führer and the Party for making Germany strong again and for our achievements in this war. I have been told that he said, "It has taken the Wehrmacht six weeks to do what it took us four and a half years to fail to do. One has to admire Herr Hitler for this."'

'He is not against this war?'

'No, sir.'

'But? There is a but?' Himmler smiled understandingly, like a benevolent priest.

'There is more than one but, sir. Although he admires the Party for having dealt with the Bolshevik threat in Germany so effectively, he believes that the Party is sometimes too close to socialism itself and that our friendship with our ally, the Soviet Union, cannot last.'

The Reichsführer nodded.

'It is also his belief that the army and particularly the officer class needs him at its head, as he was before. He believes the Führer is an effective popular leader but that our nation needs a figurehead as well.'

'Has he ever said anything disrespectful of the Party?'

Krebbs hesitated, although in no doubt where his duty lay. He had nothing against the old man – indeed, he was coming to like him, in some ways – but what was said, was said. 'He once referred to the Party as "a bunch of shirted gangsters", sir.'

When Himmler smiled his lips grew thinner and his moustache became a dark line beneath his small straight nose. 'A snobbish attitude still typical of the older generation of the officer class. Would he be interested in returning to Germany, do you think, in the absence of some titular recognition?'

'I cannot be sure, sir, but I suspect not.'

'Who reported what he said about our defeating France in six weeks?'

'One of the maids, sir.'

'And what of the Jewish question? What has he to say about that?'

'He has said that Jews and freemasons and English and American capitalism are the curse of Germany and the international system. He also said that Jews are like mosquitoes and should be gassed.'

Himmler's eyes were mild and attentive and his hands, still folded in his lap, delicate, almost girlish. He nodded faintly, as if his mind were really elsewhere. 'Is that all he has said?'

Krebbs thought. 'He believes that England, which he calls Juda-England, is in the grip of the Jews, as was Germany until the Party and the people were forced to act against them.'

'But the question prompted further hesitation in you. Has he said other things about this question or about the measures we have taken, so far, to deal with it? Does he mean what he says in this area or are his attitudes ambiguous or self-contradictory, as you have reported they are on the subject of the English?'

Fräulein Potthast was putting her underclothes and stockings in one of the drawers. Krebbs was reluctant to mention the Kaiser's remarks about the book and the remarkableness of the Jews. It was a trivial thing that would be made to sound important merely by being reported. He felt he had given a fair enough picture of the old man. 'I believe he means what he says when he says it, sir, but he does not always think about what he says and therefore it is sometimes difficult to say exactly what he would do or believe when he does think. He is a complicated man who does not know himself.'

'Did someone say this of him or is it your own assessment?'

'My own assessment, sir.' Krebbs was surprised by his own easy promptitude. He had hidden something from Schutzstaffel. Schutzstaffel, that had been so good to him, bestowing meaning, purpose, status, belief. It was a tiny thing, of course, utterly insignificant; whether it was said or not said, known or unknown, altered nothing. But the fact of hiding it made it feel like a big thing; also, what he was hiding behind it was more important. To have mentioned Akki might have provoked further questions which might have forced him to choose between revealing her secret or lying to the Reichsführer. In a sense, he was lying about her already, by omission, which just showed how corrupting was contact with Jews. He, who had always been unreservedly loyal to the cause, none more so, was being forced by the mere fact of her Jewishness to be less than completely honest with the Reichsführer himself. He would not give her away, he resolved, but nor would he continue with her. This was a lesson to him.

The Reichsführer nodded approvingly. 'So, his attitudes towards the Reich are imperfect but not dangerously unsound. His attitude towards the Party, especially its socialist mission, must be suspect. He is sound on the Bolshevik question and superficially so on the English, but sometimes ambivalent. He appears sound on the Jewish question, although his deeper attitudes have yet to be revealed or tested. In some ways, therefore, a loyal German who is anxious to serve the Fatherland, in others a preposterous old pretender who wants his throne back. What should we do with him, if anything? That is our present problem. There are also certain security questions of which you have been informed, and certain others that have arisen more recently of which you have not yet been informed.' His soft white hands, their veins prominent, were now arranged in his lap fingertip to fingertip, as in prayer. 'The information conveyed to you in signals and what I am about to say to you now comes from a most delicate source. Any unauthorised disclosure would swiftly and inevitably result in the ultimate punishment.' Fräulein Potthast was unpacking her dresses and hanging them in the wardrobe, sliding the wooden hangers carefully. The Reichsführer's mild gaze did not move from Krebbs. 'We are sure that the English leader, Churchill, wishes to invite Prince Wilhelm to defect to England and we believe, though we cannot be absolutely sure of this, that the English secret service is taking measures to establish the Prince's opinion of this matter. It is even possible that they would attempt to kidnap him if they thought such action would gain them sufficient propaganda advantage. And now there is evidence of clandestine enemy activity in this area. Not only reports, but actual evidence.'

He paused, gazing at Krebbs. His tones were as precise and confiding as before, his sentences as effortlessly bureaucratic, but his stillness seemed somehow more complete. It was as if he were absolved from, or perhaps immune to, the normal human language of gesture, emphasis and amelioration.

'Our wireless monitoring organisation,' he continued, 'has identified in this area coded short-wave transmissions of a sort used by English agents. Unfortunately, we cannot yet read them, and precise location remains difficult because they are irregular, infrequent and of short duration. It is possible that they have nothing to do with this plot against Prince Wilhelm but are concerned with the Luftwaffe headquarters, though we believe the operator – or his set – to be in or near the village of Doorn, possibly in the surrounding woods, perhaps concealed in this estate or even in this house. You have sent details of the staff here, as requested. Among them are one or two who may be worthy of further interest, in which case we shall ask you to make further inquiries pending our bringing them in for questioning. Meanwhile, you will please be vigilant for any signs of unusual behaviour, or suspicious origins or for any gossip about strangers in the area. It would be useful if – without, of course, telling them why – you could recruit for yourself a couple of sources among the estate or house workers who could keep you informed. A sensible preliminary would be the imposition of a strict regime of reporting and inspection, from which you could make discreet exception as reward for your recruited sources. Alternatively, it could provide valuable cover for seeing them privately. Is there anyone who comes to mind now either as an object of suspicion or as a suitable source?' He gazed with gentle inquiry through his gold pince-nez.

'Not immediately, sir, but I'm sure I shall find some-one.'

'I am sure you will. What of the maid who reported Prince Wilhelm's words about our defeat of France?'

'I shall start with her, sir.'

'Good.' The Reichsführer parted his fingertips so that his hands were now cupped as in benediction. He smiled enough to show his teeth, which were clean and regular. 'You may discover in yourself an aptitude for this impor-tant security work, Untersturmführer. Your reporting so far suggests this. You have seen active service already, I believe? That is good. Possibly you will wish to see more, as an SS officer should, but if things continue to go well for you here and you continue your early promise, please convey your interest through SS Standartenführer Kaltzbrunner to SS Gruppenführer Rauter, or whoever stands in for him while he is recovering from his injuries.

You perhaps have not heard that disaffected elements have attempted to assassinate him? They ambushed his car using British Sten guns. All who were with him were killed. Fortunately he survived. Severe measures will now be enacted. I shall mention our conversation to Kaltzbrunner.'

'Thank you, sir.'

The Reichsführer glanced at Fräulein Potthast, who had finished hanging her clothes in the wardrobe and was sitting on the edge of the bed, reading a magazine. Her legs were crossed and one polished brown shoe was half off, swinging slightly from her toes.

Krebbs, who had sat throughout at attention, stood and put on his cap. 'Heil Hitler!'

The Reichsführer acknowledged Krebbs's quivering salute by raising the palm of his right hand and mouthing his response, then turned towards Fräulein Potthast.

On the stairs Krebbs met Akki and another maid carrying bed linen. They backed into a corner to make way for him. He made to pass, then stopped Akki. 'Excuse me, fräulein, a word, if you please.' The other maid continued up to the landing and out of sight. Krebbs had no idea what he was going to say. Until he spoke he had intended to let Akki pass. She looked at him across the pile of linen, held before her in both hands. 'Are you all right?' he asked in a lowered voice.

'Yes. Are you?'

'I have just been with the Reichsführer. He praised me. He said very good things about me.'

'You look frightened.'

'Yes.' He surprised himself by his admission. 'When may I come and see you?'

She glanced up and down the stairs. 'Whenever I am there. But it is difficult, with others around.'

'This evening?'

99

'Maybe. But we might be busy, with so many guests. And you will be busy, surely.'

'I don't mind, you know, about what you told me. It's all right.' This was the opposite of what he had intended but, now that he had said it, he felt relieved and excited.

She glanced up and down the stairs again. 'We can't talk about it here.'

'I may come this evening, then?'

'If you like.'

'Tell the other girl I stopped you to ask about the sleeping arrangements for the Reichsführer's officers and to complain that this staircase should not be used by servants carrying things.'

She nodded and moved on.

SIX

The Princess herself inspected the dining-room before dinner that night, accompanied by the major-domo and house steward. She wore her blue and silver gown, the one she privately thought of as her coronation gown, and her most delicate gold shoes. Dinner, according to Willie's custom, was usually a plain affair. It always had been, with the Hohenzollerns. For all their tradition, they had little feel for regal living, still less for luxury. Those who did not know this probably suspected parsimony, but there would be no chance of such error on this occasion. The porcelain Neuosier dinner service was beautifully set off by the silver cutlery with its acanthus palmette decoration. That was based on the English 'King's pattern', but Herr Himmler was most unlikely to know. The candelabra gleamed and the glassware, with gilded cartouche and engraved war trophies surrounding Frederick the Great's initials, shone. The climax of the menu would be roast goose, with snails and vegetables. Herr Himmler was reportedly partial to goose.

It looked as if set out for a heavenly host, she thought as she contemplated the glittering table, and the ceiling and walls executed in scagliola. It was almost a pity to spoil the scene by eating in it, she remarked to the major-domo. She had always loved the sight of a well-laid table awaiting diners, with its sense of imminent occasion and that delicious expectancy which you wanted to prolong for ever. It was just as she liked to picture one's reception in heaven, so often described by those who had seen through death's door as a joyous banquet; though she did not remark on this to the major-domo, being troubled by the thought that he might hope to be invited.

The earthly banquet went well, she concluded later. Everyone seemed determined to be convivial and no one struck a sour note, though von Islemann was perhaps a little too quiet. Willie, in one of his smarter uniforms, was in particularly good form, laughing and talking more than usual. Herr Himmler was charm itself, so different from some of the Nazis one met. It showed, as she had more than once remarked to Willie, that the people at the top – the very top – were not only able but civilised. The adjutants were charming, too, and Fräulein Mouse was pleasant enough although, as the Princess had already gathered from friends in Berlin, she never had much to say for herself. The Princess had never met Frau Himmler but felt he could have done better for himself than the Mouse. Perhaps he was unadventurous in that respect.

The important thing, of course, was that the occasion should enhance Willie's chances of being invited to return to his throne, while at the very least securing continuance of the annual grant made to him by successive German governments. That was essential. From early in the dinner it was apparent that all was going well. While the soup was being cleared Willie described his shooting exploits to Herr Himmler, who listened with an expression of polite inquiry and without appearing too obviously bored. The light from the chandelier glinted on his pince-nez as he nodded. His lips were formed into a faint – was it faintly ironic? – smile. She resolved there and then that she really would do something for him. She was prepared already but had not, until that moment, actually decided. It always helped, if only a way could be found.

Dear Willie, meanwhile, was detailing some of the 33,967 birds and other animals recorded in his game book during his first twenty-five years of shooting. His memory was formidable still – who else could remember by heart 9,643 pheasant, 54 capercaillie, 16,188 hare, 581 'unspecified beasts', as well as all the rest – but he would keep talking over people, smothering them in mid-sentence as if unaware that they were speaking. Presumably that was one result of being Kaiser for all those years; another, of which he was equally unconscious, was always walking first through the door.

He did the first again during Herr Himmler's response to his figures, waving his fork like a conductor's baton. 'Mostly with a twenty-bore,' he said, 'resting it on the shoulder of a keeper because of my weak arm.'

It was rare for the Kaiser to refer to his arm, a sign, she thought, that he was relaxed with Herr Himmler.

'Bigger stuff with a rifle, of course,' he continued, smothering Herr Himmler's next remark. 'I tried a drilling once or twice but never got on with it. Never could. Not so much the weight as the balance. Ever tried a drilling?'

Herr Himmler had not. His hesitation led the Princess to suspect that he did not know what a drilling was. 'Willie, you cannot expect a busy man such as the Reichsführer to have time for the arcana of shooting,' she interjected. 'He has not time to play with sporting guns that are a combination of shotgun and rifle. His concern is with bigger guns than that.' She smiled at Himmler.

'They're a compromise,' the Kaiser continued. 'You need pedigree for a proper job, as in everything else.'

There were flecks of soup in his beard, she couldn't help

noticing. Herr Himmler must have noticed, too. He looked like the sort of man who noticed things and it was hard to take someone seriously when you noticed bits of food stuck to them. It was like women with flecks of lipstick on their teeth. She herself was always particularly careful about that sort of thing.

Conversation became more general with the arrival of the goose. The Reichsführer gave his views on the progress of the war. Things were going well and Germany was at last beginning to breathe deeply again. She had room to fill her lungs, no longer circumscribed by envious hostile forces seeking to confine her. But the task was far from finished, there was still so much to do and with certain important questions still unresolved every German had to be prepared to strain every sinew until victory was complete.

'But when matters in Europe are settled we shall still need a *Zollverein*, a customs union,' said the Kaiser, again cutting across what the Reichsführer was saying. 'A customs union against America, that is. That is the only way to secure European prosperity and resist American domination. And that itself is only one stage in the fight against materialism and un-German behaviour. To achieve it we must first conquer Juda-England, which has become the Trojan horse in Europe for international Jewry, American capital and freemasonry. Do you not agree, Herr Himmler?'

The Reichsführer's pince-nez glinted again as he nodded. 'The Prince speaks wisely. It is a fact that the forces that threaten German stability are the very forces that also threaten international stability. That is why there is a need for a new world order and why it is necessary to put in place certain geographic and economic changes so as to create conditions for a more spiritual, less materialist society.'

The Kaiser gestured with his fork once more, as if scattering pebbles along the table. 'And if America is foolish enough to come into the war again, as she did last time, we should repeat to them what I said then: pay us the compliment of fighting us, and we will do you the favour of solving your negro problem – send them across and we will shoot them down!'

Everyone laughed, even the Reichsführer who laughed rarely, the Princess had noticed, although his smile was near constant. 'They should pay us to do it,' added one of the adjutants.

The Kaiser raised his glass to the adjutant. 'That is a refinement of which I had not thought. We should invoice them for the ammunition. But in fact I think America is unlikely to join this war. There is no reason for them to do it this time.'

Everyone nodded. Everyone drank, too, the adjutants particularly. Even von Islemann, the Princess was pleased to note, was indulging himself a little; that was good, because he had been too subdued recently and needed to loosen up a bit. The young Leutnant Krebbs was drinking well, too, though he said little. Willie, she observed, was drinking less than appeared from his manner and gestures, certainly less than everybody else. He never drank much, anyway, but sometimes he liked to make people think he did, usually when he had something in mind. She took that as a good sign and accepted another glass herself.

'There are many Americans who would willingly honour such an invoice,' continued the Reichsführer. 'Meanwhile, we have population problems of our own, closer to home. Of course, we are all familiar with the population control methods of Genghis Khan and would feel they were a little crude for our own times, perhaps.' He smiled as he sipped his wine. One of the adjutants chuckled. 'But they may be improvable with modernisation. It is clear to all in Europe that we in Germany need room to settle about thirty million of our people. This need for *Lebensraum* – for living space, for settlement – is not controversial. What is controversial in some quarters are the policy implications of this need. There is room for such settlement only in the east but even there it would be necessary to oversee some preliminary reordering of populations. We have in fact begun this process already in Poland, though it is still in its early stages and is not widely known about, but it will be necessary to expand. Rigorous analysis indicates that development of this policy could also provide solutions to related problems, provided our actions are clearly thought-out and executed with appropriate vigour. If our policy aims prove incapable of rapid realisation and therefore call for endurance in pursuance as well as promptness in execution – as may well be the case – it is possible that we may seek various accommodations with interested international parties. In that case, it could be very helpful to the Reich' – Himmler inclined his head towards the Kaiser – 'to have the public support of certain eminent and internationally respected persons.'

The Kaiser put down his fork and raised his glass, looking directly at the Reichsführer. 'I drink to the success of the German Reich in resolving these issues and willingly pledge any help that I, or any loyal German known to me, can give.'

Himmler stood and held his glass across the table. 'To our Führer and Prince Wilhelm.' He turned to Hermine with a smile. 'And to our dear Princess.'

Everyone but the Kaiser and Hermine stood, toasted, and sat again. Conversation became livelier and more general. Obersturmbannführer Grothman, the more senior of the adjutants, leaned across to the Princess. 'It is rare for the Reichsführer to be so open,' he whispered. 'He must be feeling very good about things.'

The Princess beamed and looked across at Willie, but he was talking again. Everything was going to plan, she felt.

After the fruit – cherries, apples, strawberries, peaches and oranges, all Willie's favourites – the Kaiser decreed that men and women should adjourn together for coffee and liqueurs rather than separate. This created circumstances propitious for the most private, and riskiest, part of the Princess's plan. She had come secretly prepared but without knowing when, or whether, she would have the opportunity to enact it. In the passage leading to the Gobelin Room she drew the Reichsführer's attention to the display cases of Hohenzollern miniatures and other bits and pieces. When the others had passed into the room she broke off from her descriptions.

'I was sorry to hear of your wife's indisposition. It is not too serious, I hope?'

The Reichsführer shook his head sadly, while his lips retained the form of his smile. 'Not a threatening condition, thank you, but chronic. It comes and goes and is impossible to predict. The realisation that she would be unable to visit you and the Prince unfortunately worsened her condition. She is extremely sorry not to be here. It is most thoughtful of you to ask after her and I shall tell her of your concern.'

'I should like to do something to help, Herr Himmler, to give you something for her. Medical bills are so expensive these days, as I know to my cost, and the war has, I hear, caused shortages of certain medicines in Germany. This is necessary for the greater good, of course, but none the less it is sometimes very important to be able to get what one needs. We have only one life, after all.'

The Reichsführer nodded. 'Indeed. This is not, as has been said, the dress rehearsal.'

The Princess took a light green monogrammed envelope from her handbag. 'It would therefore please me very greatly, Herr Himmler, if you would accept this small offering on her behalf.'

The Reichsführer slipped the thick envelope into his jacket pocket with neither pause nor haste. 'You are most kind, Princess. My wife will be more than grateful.'

'It might help with some new treatment for her.'

'Of course.'

The Princess hesitated to move on, feeling she must have forgotten something and that there ought to have been more to it than that. He had pocketed the envelope as effortlessly, as seamlessly, as if it were an expected and practised thing. His action had been in keeping with the manner of her offer, but the whole transaction now seemed indecently easy. She was suddenly embarrassed, too, by the difference in height between them. She had been aware of it before, of course, but only now, as they stood in momentary silence in the passage, did it feel awkward. She was at a loss to know how to conclude, whereas he seemed unaware of the need for any conclusion. After another moment of hesitation, she moved off.

Krebbs, who had waited by the dining table as the others filed out ahead of him, watched them go. He had been an involuntary witness of the transaction, standing close to the wall out of sight, and had seen the envelope disappear into the Reichsführer's tunic pocket. As they moved away he followed, hoping it would appear he had only just come within earshot, but neither noticed him. There were two small putative boils on the back of the Reichsführer's neck, just above his uniform collar.

In the Gobelin Room the Kaiser already had his coffee, which he drank on his feet, walking about. The ladies could sit but the men had to remain standing. The Kaiser was talking again about the English. 'They have a saying about how one rotten apple will infect a whole barrel,' he said, 'but they do not realise how well it applies to themselves.

They have the Jew in their midst now. It has always been so there, at least during my lifetime, but they do not realise it, they cannot see the damage it does them. Their humour, of which they are so proud and which truly is good, so good' – he paused with his cup raised and his saucer balanced carefully in his left hand, laughing to himself – 'yes, it prevents them from appreciating that certain things are serious none the less. They laugh about international financiers and capitalism but they do not see what evil is being done.'

Everyone nodded. Krebbs, who had remained by the door, watched Akki and another maid enter the far door with liqueurs. Akki's white apron was pressed and gleaming, her face expressionless. He noticed the Kaiser following her with his eyes as she arranged glasses and bottles on a sideboard and then, at a nod from the major-domo, stood by the far door, awaiting orders. The Kaiser beckoned her to him with his cup and spoke quietly to her. She left the room by Krebbs's door, her eyes lowered.

'Now, gentlemen, liqueurs,' the Kaiser announced, handing his cup and saucer to the other maid who came forward to receive them. 'And cigars, I think.'

By the time Akki returned the air was thick with cigar smoke and drinks were being handed round. The Kaiser stood by the eighteenth-century Spindler card table, puffing on his cigar and smiling at the Princess. Akki had with her a book which, at a gesture he made with the cigar, she put on the table before him.

The Princess, Frau von Islemann and Fräulein Potthast were seated and talking among themselves. The Reichsführer was saying something to von Islemann. The other maid was serving drinks to the adjutants. After a further nod from the major-domo, Akki approached Krebbs.

'Would you like a drink, sir?'

Her grey eyes held his without a flicker. An actress, he

thought. She loves to act. Perhaps it excites her. 'A whisky, please.' It excited him.

The Reichsführer left von Islemann and turned again towards the Kaiser. 'If I may take up the Prince's point,' he said, his voice raised enough to get the company's attention, 'it is not only the English who do not appreciate the danger and insidious corruption in their midst, but also the Americans and, strangely, the Danes. Fortunately, there are people in these countries who have their eyes open and understand the problem, and these we must encourage. In some other countries there is greater awareness and consequently a greater willingness to take measures – in Poland, for instance, and in France, where co-operation with the authorities is beginning to proceed satisfactorily. Here in Holland the early signs are also promising, indicating a methodical approach to the problem. But only in Germany is there sufficient clarity of thought and courage of mind to admit the scale of the task and to confront what a final solution would involve. There has to be some adjustment of populations, and adjustment means – crucially – fewer numbers. It may surprise some people to know that I have had encouraging conversations with Jewish – yes, Jewish – leaders about this. With persistence, and under the right circumstances, even they can be persuaded of the logic of our position and hence the necessity of our solution. But we must be unceasing in our efforts to urge, persuade and explain, and for that reason – but not for that alone – we are extremely grateful for Prince Wilhelm's support, and I am happy to assure you all that the German government looks forward not only to continuing its support for Prince Wilhelm and his family but to ever closer co-operative relations in the future.'

Again, the Kaiser nodded his acknowledgement, the Princess beamed and there was a general raising of glasses, except for Krebs who still awaited his. Von Islemann, who during the Reichsführer's speech had appeared pre-occupied with the Meissen porcelain vases on the mantel-piece, folded his arms after the toast and looked down at his polished shoes, as if trying to recall something.

'And the children?' he asked quietly, before anyone else responded. 'The children of these Jewish people who have accepted the necessity for relocation and reduction?' He emphasised, by exactness rather than loudness, the last word. 'I have heard that special measures may be required to deal with children since, like the aged, the infirm and idiots, they are classified as commercially unproductive units. Is this a problem for which the Reich has identified a solution?'

The Reichsführer touched his pince-nez and turned towards von Islemann. 'This is a serious question to which we have given much thought. The relocation or disposal of economically unproductive units is at once a simple problem – in the sense that it is fundamental – and a complicated one. The answer must be as radical as the question. It must be bold and fearless. I am happy to say that we believe we have achieved it. Our method is to divide those classified as economically unproductive into two groups. In the first group are those who can, with application and with some ingenuity, be made productive. There is a surprising number of these, all of whom would have been lost to the Reich had we not thought carefully about the problem. That leaves the residue, children included, who are unsuited to any productive employment and can only be a drain on those who are. For these we have designed a system offering a merciful and rapid release.'

The only sounds in the room were the clink of ice-cubes in the water-jug and the rustle of Akki's long black dress as she crossed the carpet with Krebbs's whisky on a tray.

111

The Reichsführer sipped his own drink. 'Our experiments prove that a 5cc dose of concentrated phenol injected directly into the heart guarantees a very rapid release. Our best operator is a man I have met. He is called Oswald Kaduk. The children love him. He smiles and plays with them and gives them a red balloon which distracts their attention. Twenty-three seconds later the process is complete, the only sign being a tiny speck of blood beneath the left nipple. With his assistant, Stefan Baretzki, he can process ten a minute. They look as if they had died in their sleep.'

Krebbs hesitated over whether to add water to his whisky, deciding against. Akki, expressionless and unmoving, held the tray before him. She remained after he had indicated he wanted no water, as if she had not realised, or had simply decided to stand by him. Eventually she rustled back across the carpet.

'Thank you, Herr Himmler.' The politeness in von Islemann's voice, and his use of the Reichsführer's name, cut the silence like a stiletto. He remained with his arms folded, staring at Himmler.

The Kaiser put down his cigar and picked up the book Akki had brought him. 'So, I shall now read you some good examples of the humour of the English,' he said. The women smiled. 'The author, who is very well known in England, is called Wodehouse.'

'Indeed,' said the Reichsführer, smiling again, 'he is well known in Germany, too. We have him in Berlin. He was captured trying to escape in northern France when his car broke down. He needed his humour then, I think.'

Everyone laughed. The junior of the two adjutants, Sturmbannführer Macher, walked casually across the room to Krebbs. 'He is called von Islemann, yes?' he asked quietly.

'Yes, sir.'

Macher nodded. 'We shall remember him.'

'The book is called *Full Moon*,' the Kaiser announced. 'It is one of my favourites, featuring Lord Emsworth of Blandings Castle and the Empress of Blandings. It is very funny indeed. Listen carefully.' He read the first two or three pages in fluent but guttural English, stopping at the point where Lord Emsworth forgets the name of his own sister. He laughed and looked around. 'The scene with the Empress of Blandings is one of my favourites in all literature. It is at once absurd and believable. Just as it is quite absurd, and quite believable, that a man who is bothered by too many sisters can mistake their names. It is a sign that, deep inside, he does not wish them to exist, you see.' He chuckled and nodded. 'But perhaps not everyone here has a good understanding of English?'

No one had. 'No matter,' continued the Kaiser. 'I will read it to you again in German.'

The men stood and the ladies sat upright while the Kaiser translated, sometimes pausing between sentences to laugh, at other times explaining the humour of a phrase before repeating it to smiles and acknowledgements. When he had finished he put the book down and re-lit his cigar from a silver lighter shaped like a trumpet. 'You see?' he said, grinning through the smoke. 'No people that produces this can be all bad. At the same time, they undoubtedly need saving from their own complacency. The Empress of Blandings is, of course, a pig. But I am sure you understood that. So, best wishes, Herr Reichsführer, in your campaign against Juda-England.'

There was another general raising of glasses, with more nods and smiles.

The Kaiser then abruptly bade everyone goodnight, and took up his book again. 'I shall read this in bed tonight. Once started on a Wodehouse I can never stop. This will be my eleventh time with *Full Moon*. Goodnight.'

Puffing on his cigar, he walked in slow state from the room.

There was a feeling that the company, or part of it, had somehow been rebuked. No one commented on it, and possibly no one defined it, but the sense of it was palpable. Leave-takings were subdued and brief, though the Princess spent some time ensuring that the Reichsführer and Fräulein Potthast – to whom she made a point of being gracious – had everything they wanted.

Krebbs went outside to check the double guard he had mounted. It was raining, so he put on his cape and tramped through the puddles and wet grass to each sentry position. The window shutters were effective at blacking out the house lights, bar a few cracks and loose fittings. It would not do for enemy bombers to kill the Reichsführer by accident, as it were. After checking the house sentries he walked across the park to the gatehouse, without telephoning them in advance. There, too, he found that all was well, the guard properly mounted, with no slacking or cowering from the rain.

It rained harder during his return, angled, angry gusts like pebbles hurled in the dark, or sprays of automatic fire. No tracer this time; something to be grateful for. With his head bent against the wind, his cap pulled down over his eyes, he did not see the wrapped, hunched figure hurrying from the house towards him until they were almost on each other. Even then he did not immediately recognise him.

'A fine night for a walk, Untersturmführer,' said von Islemann. 'You are walking off the effects of dinner, perhaps?'

'Checking the guard.'

'An officer's duty is never done. I remember it well.'

It was easy to forget that Captain Sigurd von Islemann had fought in the previous war. Probably, Krebbs thought, as a staff officer who never got his knees muddy. 'What were you in?'

'Forty-eighth Infantry Regiment. Nothing as glamorous as yourself, Herr Untersturmführer. You would not have heard of us. We ceased to exist in 1917 at a place called Passchendaele. That's where I was wounded.'

'I didn't know you'd been wounded.'

A vicious gust sent their capes billowing and forced each a step back, but von Islemann seemed in no hurry. 'Your Reichsführer was very interesting after dinner, didn't you think?'

Krebbs was tempted to remind von Islemann that the Reichsführer was now his Reichsführer, too, but said nothing.

'Thought-provoking, didn't you think?' continued von Islemann loudly, almost harshly, perhaps to make himself heard above the rain.

'What he said was new to me.'

'Did it make any difference to you?'

Again, Krebbs hesitated. Von Islemann patted him on the shoulder, in unexpectedly comradely fashion. 'Don't worry, you need not commit yourself. Your silence is eloquent. Goodnight, Untersturmführer, and good luck.' He pulled his coat collar to and stepped past Krebbs into the night.

The guards outside the house challenged Krebbs correctly on his return. Back inside, in his cosy basement room, he removed his dripping cap and cape but not his boots. They might leave wet marks and they would certainly make more noise but if he were seen in uniform without his boots any explanation he attempted would be hopelessly implausible. At least if he were properly dressed he could pretend to be on some sort of duty.

His inspection had taken forty minutes but still he did not hurry. He wanted everyone else to be properly out of the way and, besides, he disliked hurrying when there was something he looked forward to, preferring to savour the anticipation. Anything connected with duty, however, or anything he disliked, he accomplished with despatch. To attack such tasks, to storm them, not only got them out of the way quickly but gave sufficient satisfaction to compensate, sometimes, for having had to do them. It was not only the savouring of anticipation that caused him to linger now, however, but anxiety that the Reichsführer's remarks about Jewish children might have upset her, and put her off.

The Kaiser, meanwhile, had gone not to his room but to his study. Although it was past his usual bedtime, he felt restless and had pains in his legs again. He knew he would not sleep yet but did not want to spend an hour or so picking over the evening with Hermine. Nor with anyone else. He rang the bell and ordered tea. It was the new girl who brought it and as soon as he saw her he felt better. This was what the doctor ordered, he thought. There was also something he wanted to clear up with her.

She put the tray on the drum table near his feet. 'Don't go,' he said. She stood looking at him, her hands clasped before her. A pretty thing, certainly, and such hands, hands such as he had never thought to feel again. 'Sit down,' he said, indicating the armchair nearest his.

After a slight hesitation, and a glance at the half-open door, she sat. She returned his smile with a small, knowing one of her own. That was enough; he was sure now that there was an understanding between them. There had been since he first set eyes upon her, he felt. He leaned forward in his chair. 'Will you be mother?'

She poured the tea. Her hands were so gentle, so deft. Their fingers touched when she passed the cup. The tea made him instantly feel better, more clear-headed, almost light-headed. 'I am very old and you are very young,' he said. 'You have nothing to fear from me, though when I was young, you would have. I would have married you just to feel your hands upon me, even though you are low-born. Well, almost married you. You know what I mean. You do not mind me saying these things?' She shook her head, still smiling, still saying nothing. 'Do you speak English?'

'Yes.'

'When I was reading I could tell you understood. It was in your eyes. Have you been there?'

'Yes.'

'And why are you here at Huis Doorn? Have you come to see me?'

'Yes.'

He smiled. It was wonderful that, in age, one could feel such happiness. 'May I hold your hand?'

She knelt at his feet and put one hand on his knee. He covered it with his right hand, stroking it and holding it gently. It was wonderful to feel that one was understood and accepted. 'I know who sent you.'

Her eyebrows raised very slightly.

'God sent you,' he continued.

'Perhaps. Not only God.'

He chuckled. 'Who, then?'

'Mr Churchill.'

'The boy Churchill? I knew him.'

'He wanted me to ask whether you would like to come and live in England.'

The clock in the corridor chimed the half hour. The Kaiser nodded slowly, squeezing her hand and looking at her. 'So, Churchill sent you with this secret invitation? I thought there was something about you. You speak like an educated foreigner. Churchill chose well, eh?' She let him fondle her hand. Perhaps this was the

117

woman behind all women, the one he had never met but always loved, the one who understood all, accepted all, demanded nothing, the woman who would take his hand in Paradise. 'But that was a bad business downstairs. It would go ill with you if they knew why you were here.'

She nodded again.

'So the Churchill boy wishes me to go to England, Hermine wishes me to return to Germany and these shirted gangsters don't know what they want of me. Well, what a problem for an old kaiser, eh? I shall have to sleep upon it. But I would prefer to dream of you.' He pressed her hand against his scarred cheek.

Krebbs could hear no one as he left his room, though a few lights were still on. He saw that the doors were locked before ascending the main staircase in order, he would explain if challenged, to check his desk outside the Kaiser's study. People had taken to leaving messages on it. There was none, as he suspected, but there was a light still on in the study and he could hear the old man speaking. His voice was lower and more subdued than usual, with none of his frequent declamatory sentences that sounded as if they ended with multiple exclamation marks. The door was ajar.

Krebbs stood, listening. It was hard to make out anything but he caught the words 'English' and 'our National Socialist friend', also, once, a phrase that sounded like 'I would tell that boy Churchill'. Huis Doorn was mentioned several times. There were indistinguishable responses from another voice, a woman's. Krebbs moved closer to the door.

It was an error to move during a pause. His belt and boots creaked and the flap of his jacket caught a pencil on his desk and sent it rolling to the floor.

'Who is there?' demanded the Kaiser, in his normal voice.

Krebbs pushed the door open. The Kaiser was seated, a cup of tea on the arm of his chair. Standing before him, dressed as she had been at dinner, her hands clasped before her, was Akki. The low light of the table lamp showed more of the Kaiser than of her; she was mainly in the shade, her white hands picked out against her black dress, her face shadowed. He had the impression, though, that her colour was higher than usual. The sense that something had just happened was sharp enough to make him pause before greeting the Kaiser. It was not possible, surely, that she would have sat in his presence, yet the cushion of the nearby armchair was indented.

'As well it is you, Untersturmführer,' the Kaiser said. 'Little Akki here has been answering my questions on how it feels to be the subject of an occupying power, and I have been trying to reassure her that Herr Himmler and his friends mean neither she nor her country any harm. But it is not always easy to be convincing, eh?' His chuckle became a snort. 'Nevertheless, I do not believe she is about to assassinate me or kidnap me.'

Akki smiled and said nothing.

'With the Reichsführer, however, it could be another matter. There are plenty who would like to assassinate him. Winston Churchill would send squadrons of bombers if he knew he was here. Already they have tried to kill that man Rauter, the SS chief in Holland. You knew about that, I presume? Two hundred and forty-three bullet holes in the SS Obergruppenführer's car. That is a serious matter. It will mean, the Reichsführer whispered to me this evening, that two hundred and forty-three Dutch prisoners will be executed, plus a few for good measure. They are thorough people, your SS, very particular as to figures. Official procedure as the simulacrum of legality, eh? I have been trying to persuade little Akki that this does not, of course, mean that innocent Dutch people are in any danger. No danger at all.'

'Will there be anything else, your Highness?' Akki asked. The Kaiser shook his head. She bobbed a curtsey and went out without looking at Krebbs.

'Sit down, Untersturmführer,' said the Kaiser, indicating the other chair. 'I have pains in my legs again this evening. It has happened several times recently. When it is bad it seems to hurt more to watch other people standing.' He pointed to the cigar box on the drum table. 'Another for me, if you please. Have one yourself.'

They were short fat cigars, mild but with a good taste. Once again the best he had ever had, Krebbs reflected; or might ever have. It felt unnatural to be seated in the presence of the Kaiser but it was something special to be smoking and talking with such a figure of history. On the same day, too, that he had sat and talked with the Reichsführer himself, a man who was making history. And later, with luck, there would be something good to come, though her downcast eyes and manner had not been encouraging. He had not known about the threatened two hundred and forty-three executions, nor about this business of the Jewish children that the Reichsführer had described. It would not be surprising if, being Dutch and Jewish, she were upset about both, but it would be unfair of her to take it out on him. He was not responsible. These were political rather than military matters. However, she had remained by his side throughout the last part of the Reichsführer's talk, when she need not have. That was possibly a good sign. He imagined undressing her.

'The visit goes well, I think,' said the Kaiser. 'Herr Hitler's Reich appears to wish us well and Hermine is pleased, which is perhaps the most important thing, eh?'

He considered his cigar. 'In one sense. In another, of course,' – his words trailed off as he watched the smoke curling and dissolving – 'there are aspects we cannot ignore. Herr Himmler's account of how they will solve the problem of hungry mouths and unproductive hands was most enlightening, very instructive. They mean business, these people of yours. Your Reichsführer has the happy knack of reducing complex problems to simple terms. Stark terms, one might say.'

'He is famed for that, your Highness.'

'A mind that sees straight through to the essentials and a temperament that is not afraid to face up to what he sees, and take appropriate action.'

'His resolve is said to be formidable.'

'A man who sees both the wider picture and the details, every one of them.'

Krebbs nodded. The Kaiser's manner appeared neither ironic nor mocking but it made him feel as if he were being played with.

'It is very important to face up to these difficult questions and achieve a final solution, once and for all. Do you agree?' The Kaiser's watery old eyes stared challengingly, as if Krebbs had been arguing.

'Yes, your Highness.'

'The Jews of Europe have to be expelled, extinguished, expunged, eradicated. I have said so myself, have I not?'

'Yes, your Highness.'

'Good boy, you will go far.'

There was a pause. The atmosphere seemed heavy with something, as if there had been a fundamental disagreement. Krebbs wondered whether he should leave.

'Tell me,' the Kaiser continued quietly, 'you have been fortunate enough to have seen action in France, as well as here in Holland a little –'

'And in Poland.'

121

'– and in Poland. What is the bravest thing you have seen done in the SS?' His tone was more thoughtful now and he contemplated his smoke again.

Krebbs thought. There were many brave things done in front-line fighting, mostly unnoticed by any except possibly a man's immediate comrades, and they did not always survive. Indeed, it was brave enough simply to stay and fight, and not run away. He remembered the day he had first come under sustained shell and mortar fire when an English brigade had counter-attacked south of Arras, driving into their flanks. It was the first time he had seen SS troopers retreat, some in panic. St Venant, which they had just taken, had to be abandoned and their neighbouring Panzer division had lost tanks and transport. It was the noise, as much as anything, that was so terrifying, the overwhelming, numbing, enveloping, disorientating noise. All you wanted to do was bury yourself or run, and it was all he could do to remain in position, to keep his men there and to keep them firing back through gaps in the smoke. They hadn't done anything spectacular that day, nothing worthy of notice, just held their ground, but each man, he knew, had found it more testing than anything else. There was nothing heroic about lying there and being shelled, your mouth dry as dust and your buttocks quivering every time you heard the whine and roar of approaching shells. Some of his men had shit themselves in their trousers. That was not a disgrace; you couldn't help it, it was like trembling, you simply couldn't control your bodily reactions. He was just grateful it hadn't happened to him.

A more obvious heroism was that of the dozen or so poor devils who had stayed to confront the English tanks when twenty broke through two fields away from his own position. With no anti-tank weapons, they had fought point-blank, some of them even jumping on the tanks to try to drop grenades down the hatches. They'd all been killed, crushed or shot to pieces every one, with no survivors to pin pretty medals on their corpses. The tanks had been comprehensively dealt with later, fortunately.

But he preferred not to talk about that, or anything else he'd actually seen; at least, not to anyone who had not been there. 'There's something I didn't witness but heard about first-hand,' he said, eventually. 'It was an officer called Kurt Meyer, who commanded a recce battalion. He was leading an advance party along a road in a valley when some rocks above were detonated by explosive charges and sent tumbling down on to the road, blocking progress. At the same time, they came under machine-gun fire from farther along the valley. They couldn't go back and they couldn't go forward. Yet if they stayed they would be killed. Meyer decided the only thing was to turn their advance into an attack. Some of them would probably be killed but if they didn't do something, all of them would be. When he ordered his men to attack, though, no one moved. It was not simply a refusal of orders, but a breakdown of comprehension. The bullets were smacking into the rocks immediately before them. He could see from their eyes when he ordered them forwards that they could not comprehend what he meant. It seemed to them like pointless suicide. So he took a grenade and shouted at everyone so that they could see him waving it. Then he pulled the pin and rolled it behind the last man.' Krebbs smiled. 'He said he had never seen such a concerted leap forwards. They all jumped as if bitten by tarantulas. They made it to the next cover, and the next, and so on. The spell was broken. They were grinning and laughing at each other now. Most of them survived.'

The Kaiser nodded. 'That must be the epitome of your Waffen SS culture, what you all aspire to. It is the kind of action that wrests victory from the impossible and the effect on the morale of your enemies spreads wider than any individual action. They believe they have lost before they meet you. But it is also wasteful. Your best troops pay a high price in butchers' bills, which could become difficult if this war lasts as long as the last. Remember 1916. The French holding Verdun, and our holding the British on the Somme, was a cost – in NCOs particularly – from which we never recovered. And you train with live ammunition, don't you? That is wasteful, too.'

Relaxing now into the kind of conversation he liked, Krebs sat back in his chair and even crossed his legs. 'It is true, there are losses. But it is done so that we in the SS are more accustomed to using our weapons under adverse conditions and to being within fifty to seventy metres of the explosions of our own artillery fire than any other troops. So the shock of battle is not so great for us.' Yet it had been shock enough, that day when they were held up outside Dunkirk by the English Guard regiments who had, in the words of his division's battle report, 'fought magnificently and grimly to the death'. His division had lost a hundred and fifty men dead on that day alone. They had fought bravely, however, overcoming the English, which would have been harder without such demanding training. 'The Reichsführer himself has acknowledged the costliness of this training and regrets the loss of each soldier but he pointed out that every drop of blood spilled in training saves streams of blood in battle.'

'Very possibly. But it is easy to say that sort of thing. We are persuaded by our own rhetoric. Has he seen action himself, your Reichsführer?'

'Not yet.' It was a weak, foolish reply and he was angry with himself for it. He had said the first thing to come to mind in order to avoid the obvious response, which was – have you? Or – he has seen as much action as you, your Highness. It angered him that he should so easily make himself look foolish in order to spare the feelings of this preposterous old man.

But the Kaiser puffed on his cigar and said nothing, staring at the tea-tray on the drum table. The pause lasted so long that Krebbs wondered whether the Kaiser had forgotten his presence. His own two last words seemed to hang in the smoky air between them.

'And what is the worst thing you have seen?' the Kaiser asked. The expression in his eyes was hard to make out. 'I mean, the worst thing that you have seen done by men of the SS?'

'Nothing,' was what Krebbs wanted to say, but he held his tongue. It was not easy, it depended what was meant, how you defined it, whether you made allowances for war. In Poland, certainly, he had witnessed arbitrary brutalities, casual killings of civilians, the clumsy bayoneting by two guards of a limping prisoner-of-war who was holding up the column, though he had committed none himself. He had been surprised by these things but had not permitted them to affect him, had not dwelt on them. It was his first taste of war and he had not known what to expect; it was not clear what was normal and his desire, as always, was to find the norm and conform to it. So he had waited to see. Since then he had seen more fighting. Things happened, as soon as they had they were in the past and, once they were, there was nothing you could do. Days and nights followed in a seamless phantasmagoria of action and inaction, of weariness, privation, duty, routine and waiting, always so much waiting. What had happened yesterday might have been in another life, as remote from today as the unknowable events of tomorrow.

Krebbs did not want to answer the Kaiser's question directly; doing so would entail a detachment that belied how events were experienced, that ignored their over-whelming pressure, the irresistible current that swept you along among them. It would be to pretend he could somehow detach himself from his own life, while the flow of his life continued. The truth was, there was no worst, only different bad things at different times and places, for different reasons, in different circumstances. He supposed the Kaiser was going to go on about the proposed two hundred and forty-three executions in revenge for the bullets in Rauter's car. Well, that was SS security police business, nothing to do with the fighting soldiers of the Waffen SS.

'Were you at Le Paradis?' asked the Kaiser.

The question opened up the feeling beneath Krebbs's thoughts like the welling-up of blood behind a surgeon's knife.

'You may wonder how I know about it,' continued the Kaiser. 'It is surprising what I hear. People tell me things simply because I am Kaiser. They think I should know, or do know, and they want to tell somebody, especially something like that. It was in France, of course, not here, but nevertheless I heard about it because the SS did it and the Wehrmacht discovered it, and they talk about it, and some of those Wehrmacht officers have relatives who visit me. Two of the English soldiers survived, you see, and were found by the Wehrmacht and taken to hospital. One day the world will know. Were you there?'

'I was there afterwards.' That was why he had not counted it the worst thing he had seen. He had not seen it done. It was a reasonable argument so long as he did not think too much about it.

'What did you think when you saw it?' The Kaiser spoke gently, almost kindly.

'At first I couldn't make out what had happened.' The mere acknowledgement made Krebbs feel freer. The little farm near Paradis was more vivid to him now than in the confused state in which he had first come across it, towards dusk that evening when bringing his company out of the line. Their new commander, Obersturmführer Fest, had been blinded during the fighting against the English Guard regiments. They had been in action for thirty-six hours and were exhausted, barely able to put one foot before another, and he kept having to stop, not only to rest but to refresh his failing memory from the map. He had the grid reference of battalion headquarters but had to concentrate even to grasp the numbers, let alone envisage the route. He was dazed with tiredness and the map symbols moved while he stared at them. In fact, they were off their route in coming to the farm but he thought there might be water there. They could rest for ten minutes, set a new route and still make HQ by dusk.

The British 4th Brigade had made a stubborn final stand to permit the remnants of the English army to escape from Dunkirk. They had achieved their objective, at great cost to themselves. Now their survivors, exhausted like their attackers, nearly all of them wounded and virtually out of ammunition, had surrendered. From a few bodies they passed on the way to the farm, Krebbs saw that this regiment was called Royal Norfolk. The bodies, heaps and bundles of brown rags carelessly discarded by hedges, half in, half out of ditches, hunched and sprawling, gaping and peaceful, often incomplete or strangely broken, were numerous enough to suggest a serious engagement. They were interspersed, in upsetting numbers, by similar bodies in field grey, bearing the regimental flashes of the 2nd SS Totenkopf Infantry Regiment. There was nothing more moving than the sight of one's own dead, nothing more capable of lighting anger even in the ashes of spent men. It was not a demonstrative anger but a quiet, sullen determination to avenge, if necessary to annihilate. As they entered the farmyard the blanket of exhaustion that all but smothered each man was lifted a fraction.

Nothing much was happening. A few soldiers were moving lethargically about, presumably on non-urgent tasks, there was a field ambulance near the house, a lorry and light field gun beyond it. The lorry engine was on tick-over and some medics were collecting German bodies on stretchers and laying them in a row on the ground before a large barn. Krebbs could not help counting; seven so far, another added while he halted his men, two more coming in. In the yard, before the open doors of the great barn, was a heap of British rifles and other weapons, with boots and bits and pieces of their equipment lying nearby. He asked a corporal he recognised, one of Obersturmführer Fritz Knochlein's 4th company, if there was any water, and was directed to a trough around the corner of the barn.

Nothing had prepared him for what they found there, not the weary indifference of the soldiers moving about the quiet farmyard nor the brown cow and her calf drinking slowly and deeply from the stone trough, water dripping from their mouths when they raised their heads to gaze passively at the newcomers. At the foot of the barn wall lay a long, untidy heap of bodies in brown, some in startling, spread-eagled attitudes, open-mouthed and open-eyed at the sky, others hunched or curled, hands and boots protruding at odd angles, one muddied and bloodied leg across another's face here, the head of a pale, fair-haired boy sticking out under somebody's arm there. About thirty metres away and ten metres apart were two small piles of spent cartridge cases, lent a dull shine by the setting sun. Spandau machine-guns, Krebbs could tell. The old red brick of the barn wall was spattered and pock-marked at about chest height.

Someone revved the lorry engine, someone else shouted and they heard it pull grindingly away. The cow left the trough and picked her way around the edge of the heap with ungainly precision, avoiding outstretched limbs and upturned helmets, followed by her calf. Before she was quite away from the bodies, she stopped, humped her back and urinated in a great splashing arc, wetting several of them. House martins darted in and out of the eaves of the barn. When Krebbs looked round he saw his entire company gathered in silence behind him.

'I thought it was bad,' he continued eventually. 'We all did, in my company. It was not – not soldier-like. Not proper work for soldiers. That's what we thought.'

'No, indeed,' said the Kaiser, still gently. 'A truly terrible thing. So unnecessary. As for shooting and bayoneting the survivors, no one likes that. Except that they missed the two I mentioned and they were found by the Wehrmacht unit that came by that evening. That is how we know what happened, that these one hundred men of Norfolk – I have been there, of course, my uncle had a house there – surrendered when they had held the line for as long as they were ordered and their ammunition had run out. They were disarmed, marched around the corner of the barn, lined up and machine-gunned. All on the orders of the officer commanding that company. That is not, I imagine, how the SS likes other armies to remember it, eh? Not the kind of battle honour that you, Untersturmführer, are proud of, eh?'

The old man put his cigar to his lips and made it glow. Krebbs realised that his own had gone out. 'Knochlein, the officer commanding that company, is not popular,' he said. 'Some have talked of challenging him to a duel and some soldiers have complained of unsoldierly practices and have requested transfers. But he is still there.' He sounded to himself as if he were speaking loudly and forcefully. 'I am glad I was not there to see it,' he said, with deliberate slowness. 'We are not proud of it. It is not what we would like to be known for.'

'So, an aberration, then?' asked the Kaiser, softly.

'Yes, your Highness. An aberration.'

'That is what you really think, eh? An exception, not part of SS culture? Something different, nothing to do with you, just as what your Reichsführer was saying about the little children was also nothing to do with you? That is what you think, eh?' As the Kaiser spoke his voice gathered energy. He put his cigar in his mouth, leaned forward and, gripping the arm of his chair with his right hand, pushed himself upright. His face reddened with the effort but when Krebbs got up to help he motioned him brusquely away. 'Save your energy for your struggle,' he muttered, and hobbled from the room.

Krebbs listened to the old man shuffling along the carpet in the corridor. 'Do not get old,' he remembered his grandfather saying. 'Old age is not for sissies.' He smoked his cigar for some minutes after he could hear no more, then stubbed it. The smell, if he had taken it with him, would have permeated the attic. It would probably cling to him anyway, but no matter. He made his way to the attic stairs, treading carefully past the closed door leading to the Reichsführer's apartment. It provoked in him an unwanted image of the Reichsführer's profile, his chin receded so much that the entire lower half of his face appeared to retreat, leaving the upper half bulbous and top-heavy. An unsatisfactory profile.

He paused to listen at the bottom of the stairs. There were no lights and no sounds. He trod slowly on each uncarpeted stair, conscious of every creak of his boots. At the top he paused again. He had unusually good night vision, though his eyes were still adapting. SS trainers reckoned it took about thirty minutes to adapt fully. There was, anyway, a slither of light showing beneath her door, though not from any of the others. That was encouraging. Holding his breath and moving on the balls of his feet, he stepped across and felt for the handle. A knock, even a soft knock, might awaken others. He turned it slowly and stepped in.

The light came from her bedside lamp which stood, as before, on the kitchen chair. The red alarm clock was there, too, but not the Dutch novel. The mirror and washbasin were still propped up on the chest of drawers, her spare clothes hung on the door hook, the eaves cupboard door had come open again and showed the brown suitcase. But there was no Akki.

The bed was undisturbed and cold to the touch. The stout black shoes that had been on top of the suitcase were gone and her lighter shoes were by the door. There was no coat on the door hook. He had been prepared for resistance, acquiescence, angry emotion or sleep, but not for absence. Perhaps she had a boyfriend in the village after all, though his guards had orders to report any-one trying to leave the grounds. He resented her for not being there, as though she had broken a promise. He assured himself he had an official reason for seeing her: his duty to report what the Kaiser had been saying to her about the war. That made absence all the more reprehensible. He sat on the bed, acknowledging, while refusing to contemplate, the possibility that she might be out all night, without permission. Doing what, and with whom, was something he did not want to think about. The only sound was the metallic ticking of her red clock.

It was perhaps that that prevented him hearing her approach. Quite suddenly she stood in her stockinged feet in the doorway, dripping wet in her long dark coat and felt hat. In one hand she held the smaller brown suitcase, in the other her shoes.

They stared at each other without speaking, then she stepped in and quietly closed the door. She put her case down carefully, and hung her hat and coat on the hook. Her movements were slow, as if in the extremity of weariness, or as if each required careful thought. She still wore her long black maid's dress, the hem of which was wet. Water dripped from her coat to the floor. She stepped across to the chest of drawers and started doing something with her hair in the mirror, as if she were trying to pretend he was not there. When he looked at her reflection, however, she gave a small smile.

'Is it not polite to stand when a lady comes into the room, Untersturmführer, especially her own room? Or do you not consider me a lady?'

He glanced at the clock, grinning despite himself. Her playfulness was an inexpressible relief, like a reconciliation. 'Ladies should not be out after midnight. What were you doing?'

'Hiding in the woods and signalling to the enemy.'

Strand after strand of hair dropped upon her shoulders as she removed hair-pins and put them on the chest of drawers. When they were all out she shook her hair, held it in a pony's tail and brushed it vigorously. He went to her, took the brush from her hand, put it on the chest of drawers and embraced and kissed her. After a moment's resistance, during which she tried to say something, she responded. This time, he felt, there would be no holding back.

But she soon broke off, pushing her head into his chest, then standing back and shaking it. 'No, Martin, I cannot, with you in this uniform.'

'I'll take it off.'

He started to unbuckle his belt but she gripped his wrist, staring at its motto. 'My Honour is my Loyalty,' she read aloud. Holding his wrists and still shaking her head, she rocked herself backwards and forwards against him. 'I like you in it, it is you, Martin, and I hate it, that's the trouble.

You understand, don't you? After what your Reichsführer was saying about the best ways of killing Jewish children? That is what he stands for and what his uniform stands for. His uniform is your uniform. It is what you stand for, too.'

'I don't, I don't think it's right to kill children. The Reichsführer is wrong.' He heard himself as if from outside himself, as once when he had been hot and cold with influenza and his own voice had sounded disembodied. 'I do not agree with it. I would not do such things.'

'But you are part of it.'

'I am not, really, Akki. Yes, I am part of SS but as a soldier of SS, Waffen SS, fighting other soldiers. What happens in the camps, in security, in all these other parts is nothing to do with us. We are for proper warfare, army against army. We have nothing to do with other business. What we do is honourable.'

'Like Paradis?'

So she too knew about it. Did the whole world know? Could she have heard it from the Kaiser, or he from her? They obviously talked to each other with unusual intimacy. 'Paradis was wrong, too,' he said.

She let go of his wrists. 'How can you be an SS officer and a Jew-lover? What would your soldiers say to that, or your colleagues, or your Reichsführer?'

'I don't care if you are a thousand times a Jew, Akki. I don't care what the Reichsführer thinks. For me it doesn't matter any more. Until now, I never knew any Jews, apart from one boy at school but that was different. Now you have opened my eyes. I see differently now. It doesn't matter for me, really.' He had never spoken like this, especially not to a girl, nor even had such thoughts before he spoke them. It was speaking that brought them into being. Everything was coming together, or coming apart. Condemning the Reichsführer was an apostasy that felt like liberation. His own words made his skin tingle. His throat tightened on them as he finished. He took hold of her shoulders.

She fingered the sleeves of his uniform. 'And think what it is for me, a Jewess whose country you have invaded, to be the lover of the brutal occupier. You cannot say these things don't matter. Even if they did not to us, they would to everyone who knows us.'

His eyes rested on the small suitcase she had left by the door. 'What were you talking about with the Kaiser this evening and what were you really doing outside?'

'I told you.' She whispered the words in his ear, her arms around his neck as she pulled him to her.

Afterwards, although he tried often, he could not recall the night in detail. They slept little, if at all, and talked much, or so it seemed. Their talk was as passionate as their physical engagement, and as hard to recall precisely. But there were a few exchanges that stood out from the night with hard, isolated clarity, their contexts vague, or lost. One, he remembered, was about the Kaiser. It was still dark, with not enough light to show the window.

'Were you sitting with the Kaiser when I came in?' he asked.

'He invited me to sit.'

'He is very informal with you. He must like you.'

'He likes my hands.'

He took one and kissed it. 'Would he like to do this?'

'He would if I let him.'

'Has he tried?'

'You're not jealous of the Kaiser, are you?'

'I am jealous of everything you touch. Other people, your own clothes, dinner plates, your hairbrush, door-knobs, everything. But what was he talking about? I heard him talking.'

'He was considering what to do.'

'About what?'

'Germany and England.'

He recalled no more of that. There was another exchange, when the pre-dawn pallor had lightened the edges of the window behind the shutters.

'Some things are indivisible,' he remembered her saying, with slow distinction. 'You must not think me an exception. I am not, I am one of them. Nor can you think that the SS is good except for its treatment of Jews. That is the mouthful of seawater that gives you the taste of the ocean. It encapsulates all that the SS and the Nazi Party stand for. That is why you cannot be truly good, and a true Nazi. And why you cannot be the Martin I could like and Untersturmführer Krebbs, SS. You have to be one or the other.'

'Is this what you were saying to the Kaiser?'

'He knows it.'

'He does not like Jews. He blames them for everything.'

'He understands indivisibility. That is why he is troubled.'

Later, or possibly soon after, he felt, or dreamt he felt, that he was trussed and bound in strong silk. He didn't mind – it was quite pleasant – but he was being used for something, and wanted to know for what. He asked, or dreamt he asked, 'What are you really doing here?'

'I am here to discover what the Kaiser wants.'

He had a vague memory of himself saying, 'That's all right, then,' or something like it. Then it was morning, with sparrows squabbling on the window-ledge. He carefully extricated himself from the narrow bed and hurried into his uniform, keen to get downstairs and shave before anyone saw him. She awoke only when, dressed, he knelt by the bed.

She put her arms around his neck. 'This cannot be, Martin, for either of us.'

'But I can come again tonight?'

'Of course.'

The kitchen staff were already about but he reached his room without being seen. He was late for his morning inspection and shaved hastily, cutting himself because he hadn't bothered to tighten the blade in its holder. One corner neatly parted the skin in two parallel lines and it took an unconscionable time to staunch the dribbles of blood. There was then no time to get coffee from the kitchen, still less breakfast. When he made his inspection he could see that the corporal of the guard had to make an effort not to remark on the two thin slashes. At least his uniform collar would hide any bite-marks on his neck.

Krebbs had finished his inspection and the house-party was still at breakfast when a despatch rider arrived with an urgent signal for the Reichsführer. Krebbs knocked and took it in, saluting and then handing the sealed envelope to Sturmbannführer Macher.

'Good morning, Untersturmführer. A matter of honour, I trust, involving a lady, eh? Not like my own, I confess.' The Kaiser laughed, gesturing with his fork at Krebbs's scars, his mouth full of toast and specks of jam in his beard. 'Duels for honour are very well but those for the honour of women are better still. I trust you were protecting the lady? A gentleman should always be on that side.'

The others smiled. The Reichsführer opened the envelope, read the signal quickly and handed it back, still open, to Macher. 'Thank you, no reply,' he said pleasantly.

Krebbs saluted again and left. Later, while he was confirming transport arrangements for the party's departure, he was summoned to the Reichsführer's room. Himmler sat at the small desk, as before, while Fräulein Potthast packed. He held the signal in one hand and smiled at Krebbs, but did not invite him to sit.

'I wish to thank you, Untersturmführer, for helping to

make our stay so happy and useful. Your briefing on our host's attitudes and predispositions was particularly helpful. You will recall the security matter I discussed with you yesterday?' He held up the signal. 'Here is further evidence of clandestine enemy activity in this area. There was another transmission last night, almost certainly a field cipher transmitter of a sort issued to certain kinds of British agent. We know them well; we have captured examples. The cipher used remains unreadable, so far, and the operator was disciplined enough to keep his transmission time within the limits the enemy recommends. Fortunately, however, the enemy underestimates our direction-finders who were able to locate the transmission site to within a half-kilometre square with Huis Doorn at its centre. It is possible that the site was actually within this house, or within its grounds.' He handed the signal to Krebbs. 'You may keep it, in a secure place, of course. There may be others before you capture this agent or traitor. He must be caught, and quickly. If you can help it would be a considerable feather in your cap, doubtless leading to promotion.'

Krebbs took the signal. 'Very good, sir.'

'Where is the house of von Islemann?' the Reichsführer asked, with no change of tone.

'In the village, sir, just outside the grounds.'

'Within half a kilometre?'

'As the crow flies, sir, yes.'

'I should like a full report on von Islemann, his background, duties, personal characteristics, political sympathies, family connections, friends, travels abroad, religious beliefs and financial dealings.'

Krebbs listened with a growing emptiness in his stomach that had nothing to do with hunger. The signal in his hand gave the transmission times as while he was waiting for Akki the night before. She had been out, in the woods, in the rain. Signalling to the enemy, she had told him, smiling.

'And I should be grateful for your own impressions of him,' the Reichsführer continued. 'Anything, no matter how trivial. Put them in a separate paragraph and let me have the complete report within two days.'

'Very good, sir.'

'If you can make a significant contribution to this case, Untersturmführer, your career in our security branch – should you wish – would be off to a very good start.'

'Thank you, sir.'

The Reichsführer stood and put on his cap, the size and breadth of which again emphasised his receding chin and disappointing lower face. He continued smiling. 'And now I must consider what would be an appropriate birthday present for the Italian ambassador. Heil Hitler!'

'Heil Hitler!' Krebbs saluted, clicked heels and left the room.

SEVEN

Krebbs stood next to von Islemann as the Reichsführer's green BMW and its escort accelerated down the drive towards the gatehouse. The household had come to the foot of the steps to see him off and the Princess waved until both cars were out of sight, though the Kaiser turned away and began mounting the steps as soon as the doors had closed. Von Islemann remained, his hands behind his back, gazing after them.

He turned to Krebbs. 'How did you find your Reichsführer? Was he anything like you expected?'

'He was friendlier than I had expected, less formal.'

'It is true he smiles a lot. But is that enough, do you think?'

'It has helped him to become popular in higher circles.'

'Perhaps it has. But I believe other qualities are also necessary in those exalted regions.'

Krebbs said nothing. Von Islemann still lingered, looking after the now-vanished car. 'Did the Reichsführer form a good opinion of His Highness, do you think?'

'So far as I could tell, he enjoyed his stay. His thoughts are not easy to read.'

'You saw more of him than I. Is it your impression

that he had no immediate plans to do anything about His Highness's situation here, either way?' The question was asked casually, as if it were an afterthought.

Krebbs hesitated. 'It was my impression that in most situations the Reichsführer would prefer not to do anything provided things are working smoothly and comfortably for him and provided he sees no threat.'

Von Islemann turned again to Krebbs. 'That is fortunate. His Highness is anyway determined to die here at Doorn, whatever invitations he has. Or from whomsoever.' He looked deliberately at Krebbs as he spoke the last few words. 'It is important that people understand that.'

Von Islemann went on leave later that day. Krebbs had known nothing of it in advance but it made his task easier, in that he could question servants and other staff about him by pretending it was part of a routine form-filling exercise that von Islemann himself would have completed were it not for the interruption of the Reichsführer's visit and, now, his absence. He decided he would not question the Kaiser or the Princess for fear of drawing attention to what he was doing.

He did not, in fact, want to write the report at all, though it was a useful distraction. Increasing familiarity had not bred in him any particular liking for the aloof, efficient private secretary who, with his quiet manner and aristocratic background, seemed by his very unassertiveness to assert an unspoken superiority. That the Kaiser trusted him completely was obvious from the way he spoke to him without addressing him, as though he were a familiar piece of furniture, always there. Krebbs had assumed that von Islemann had no particular liking for himself, as the working-class product of the new socialism, thrust upon the household in a position of some power. Hitherto they had been correct with each other rather than friendly, and during the hurried arrangements for the Reichsführer's visit they had co-operated efficiently but without warmth or humour. During their encounter in the park the previous night, however, and again during their exchange that morning, von Islemann's manner had been more friendly, more confiding, as if he and Krebbs shared a secret, or at least certain assumptions. It discomforted Krebbs but he could not resist responding, and at the same time it flattered him.

Similarly, von Islemann's quiet, unafraid questioning of Himmler about the arrangements for Jewish children had both increased Krebbs's respect for him and made him uneasy. His unease was not only that the questions might have provoked a scene or argument – might even have been construed a breach of manners – but they had made him feel that he personally had something to be guilty about. There was nothing he should feel guilty about, he told himself, he had nothing to do with that side of things; it was nothing to do what he did, no matter what Akki said. But still he felt it, and it made him the more uneasy that von Islemann appeared to be taking to him.

It also made it hard to say anything definite about the man's political attitudes, without resorting to surmise. For the first time since joining the SS he had been given a task that made him uncomfortable. In abstract, reporting on a man's political attitudes was a perfectly reasonable thing to do, particularly during a struggle for national survival when loyalty was essential. In practice, though, when you worked daily alongside a living being, manifold, elusive, with so much unknown, it seemed dishonest to pronounce with certainty upon anything. His discomfort was sharpened by the reactions of others. When he asked the cook how long von Islemann had worked for the Kaiser, her dignified response to the effect that such questions were best answered by His Majesty, who knew best what was proper to ask and answer, caused a spasm of shame which he masked beneath a veneer of bureaucratic indifference.

And all the time he was sure the exercise was unnecessary. It was not von Islemann that they – or he – needed to worry about.

Nevertheless, he had to write the report and there was little time to do it. Eventually he asked the Princess, explaining that it was just a question of keeping his records up to date. She was in the rose garden, a basket on her arm, secateurs in hand and a gardener in attendance. 'For ever,' she answered indifferently. 'He was with Willie when I first came. You will have to ask Willie.'

Very soon it seemed to Krebbs that every answer, from whomsoever and to whatsoever, was accompanied by a suggestion of contempt. His own manner hardened and he became more officious, yet still he held back from approaching the Kaiser or Akki.

He was at his desk when the Kaiser, whom he thought asleep, emerged abruptly from his study with an unlit cigarette between his fingers. It was hard to tell from his look whether he was more surprised or displeased to see Krebbs. 'The Princess informs me that you are asking about von Islemann.'

'I have been ordered to complete the records of the household, your Highness.'

'By Himmler?'

'By the Reichsführer, yes.'

'Von Islemann has been with me since before I came into exile. He has been exemplary throughout. He is a loyal German officer. I have the highest opinion of him. There is no other member of my staff whom I value more.' He held his cigarette before Krebbs. 'I find neither lighter nor matches in my study today. Bring me some.' He went in and closed the door.

Domestic errands were no part of Krebbs's duty. He was

not a servant, was not attached to the Kaiser's staff. HQ SS would undoubtedly support him if there were a row about it. At the same time, he had the habit of obedience and took positive pleasure in the prompt and efficient execution of orders. Nor did he dislike the old man, unreasonable and inconsistent though he was. He found a lighter that worked, a heavy little piece modelled on an antique field gun, and took it in.

The Kaiser, who was sitting with a book, put it carefully on the arm of his chair after lighting his cigarette. 'A memento of the 1870 war,' he said, 'when we were wise enough to fight only the French. What would that old fox, Bismarck, have to say to this present business, I wonder?' He groaned as he shifted in his chair. 'My pains again, damn them. "Balance your friends and enemies," he would say. "Choose each carefully." Well, have we done that, do you think? Are we doing it now?' His eyes bulged slightly.

'We are in alliance with Russia this time, your Highness, instead of against her.'

'Alliance with the Bolsheviks? What is it worth, an alliance with the people who murdered my cousin the Tsar and his family, and all his little ones, too? What is the value of an alliance with people for whom blood is the argument of first and last resort? And what of us, in that respect? It will be a race to see who breaks this alliance first, if what Herr Himmler said about the east is anything to go by.' He stared at the unlit fire. 'Yes, and then when I am gone and your task here is ended you may find yourself on a new eastern front, my good Untersturmführer. A different kettle of fish to life here at Huis Doorn, as the English would say, eh?'

'I hope to acquit myself well wherever I am sent, your Highness.'

'I am sure you do and sure you would. A soldier's duty

is to do his duty, no more, no less. He is a monk in arms. But Russia is very big, especially when you are still at war in the west. We did it, remember. But that was before the Bolsheviks took over. And remember Napoleon, too. He failed, yet he, like Herr Hitler, had swept all before him. And he failed with the English, too.'

He continued staring into the neatly stacked kindling wood, logs and coal, as if his thoughts could be read there and need no longer be spoken. Krebbs made to withdraw.

'It is colder today,' the Kaiser continued, without looking round. 'Unless it is just me. Have someone light the fire, would you?'

Krebbs was kept busy during the middle part of the day, prevented from starting his report by an urgent and pointless demand from battalion headquarters for an inventory of all their rations, kit and weapons, to be sent back with the next ration lorry, arrival time unknown. It was the infuriating sort of paperwork that lower formations blamed on High Command's having nothing better to do, and that High Command was forever calling on lower formations to reduce. Its urgency was probably due to battalion HQ having ignored it until the deadline was imminent. He also had to rearrange the guard rosters since five men were due home leave.

He was aware, of course, that at any turn of the corner he might run into Akki but, for the time being, he almost didn't want to. He was still digesting his memories of the night before, some of which he preferred not to think about directly but to circle round and explore, as it were, by feel. Seeing her might throw everything he was beginning to order into turmoil.

The house was quiet after lunch and he became more aware of his lack of sleep. Unusually, the Kaiser had gone out to chop wood, which he normally did in the mornings, and the sounds of his axe came through Krebbs's open window. The intervals were longer than usual; perhaps the old man was tired, too. The only other sounds were the chiming of the household clocks – less ragged, thanks to Krebbs, but far from simultaneous – and the occasional splash and protest of ducks in the moat. The sun was veiled by cloud and the air felt like rain.

Akki came to him while he was sitting at his desk pondering how to start his report on von Islemann, and waiting for the next fall of the Kaiser's distant axe. He didn't realise she was behind him until she spoke.

'I've never seen you so still, not even in your sleep. You were restless then.'

He stood, smiling with relief at seeing her, despite everything. 'I wasn't aware I had slept. Did you?'

'Probably, but it didn't seem like it.'

She wore her day dress and carried a feather duster and dustpan and brush. They spoke in undertones and stood well apart, although there was no one nearby. His concerns about what was happening were not vanquished by her presence, merely pushed to the periphery. They remained real enough but when she was there they seemed less important. In his mind, though he tried not to show it in word or gesture, he happily surrendered to her.

'You are having to report on von Islemann?' she asked.

'You have heard about that?'

'Is he in trouble?'

'He may be. It depends on what I say.'

'Because of the questions he asked the Reichsführer?'

'I suppose so.'

'Nothing else?'

'That's enough, I think. What else were you thinking of?'

'Nothing. You.'

He stepped across and kissed her. She smiled as she rearranged her dress. 'You're so ardent, yet you always look so cool and official.'

'You're so articulate, yet you always look so meek and maid-like.'

'Of course I'm maid-like, I'm a maid.'

'Better educated, though. More sure of yourself.'

'We have better schools in Friesland.' She turned to go into the Kaiser's study.

He folded his arms and leant against the wall, blocking her. 'Why are you so worried about von Islemann?'

She looked at him, unsmiling now. 'It's not only him, what happens to him. It's that someone like you can believe in and follow someone as evil and grubby as your Reichsführer.'

His arm muscles stiffened, but he did not move. It was dangerous to talk like that, even in undertones, dangerous for him to hear it. 'What makes you think I am so different?'

'It's obvious you find dishonesty and disloyalty difficult, although you know in your heart it may be right to be so. As for Himmler and his henchmen, you have eyes and ears, even if you don't want to use them.'

Once again he could not help picturing the Reichsführer pocketing the Princess's envelope. It made him angry with Akki. 'You seem to think you know me better than I know myself.'

'I do not, Martin. That is my point. You know the truth about yourself and these people, really. You are better than them. I have sensed that in you since we first spoke. It is why I like you. If you cleave to them they will absorb and destroy you.'

'And you learned to speak like this in your hamlet in Friesland?'

At the sound of footsteps on the stairs he straightened

and moved away. She went into the Kaiser's empty study with her duster, while he collected his papers and rang through to the gatehouse to say he was coming down.

He wrote his report there, undisturbed. It was not easy to write as if there were something to say while at the same time saying nothing very much. No one in the household reported anything of von Islemann that was remotely bad or threatening to him: his political opinions were unknown since he never voiced them; his work for the Kaiser was a model of discretion, exactitude and courtesy; his advice to his master was never offered unless asked for and tended always to be cautious and sensible, urging restraint; the Kaiser, though he sometimes huffed and puffed, invariably took it. His relations with the staff were formal but cordial; for one often remote in manner, he was surprisingly popular. People sensed fairness and integrity, perhaps also an underlying kindness. The inwardness of his marriage and family life was unknown but from the externals it appeared quiet and content; at least, well organised.

Little was known of his background. Military gentry, aristocratic, of course, the Kaiser would know, or the Princess. He had travelled with the Kaiser to the Kaiser's house on Corfu, where the Kaiser practised his archaeology, but it was not known whether he had made other overseas trips or had foreign friends, apart from local Dutch friends of his wife's. He spoke fluent Dutch to his wife and it was assumed he spoke French and possibly some English, but no one knew. It was true that he had fought in the last war. He had had a good war, people said.

'He would have been a good priest, or a scholar,' the major-domo added, after Krebbs had finished questioning him. 'He has a conscience and scruples. He is honest. He always wants to get things right. That is, to see things clearly and fairly and to be exact about them. Of what is happening now in Germany or in this war he never speaks, except that when he told us who our guest was he said we should use the best silver but count it afterwards. But that was just a joke, I think.'

It was the kind of joke that the Sicherheitsdienst, the SS security department, liked to hear about. Krebbs knew enough of them to know that. One man had disappeared from his training course after making a joke about the Führer suggesting he could not give a woman children. All von Islemann's studied rectitude, his assiduous propriety, his caution, his loyalty to Germany, would count for nothing if the Sicherheitsdienst were given that stick to beat him with. This, along with his questioning of the Reichsführer, would be sufficient to constitute an attack on the Reich, a plot against the state involving not only von Islemann himself but his wife and children and any friends within reach. At the same time, the career of Untersturmführer Krebbs would benefit greatly by the uncovering of such a plot. There would be promotion and a prestigious headquarters post. He would have more money, would meet more women, be more attractive to more of them. But not to all.

On the other hand, if he did not report the joke and it were subsequently discovered that he had not, he might be assumed to be part of the plot. Whatever he did now, therefore, was bad. 'That is the fault of the system you serve,' he imagined Akki saying. He thought for a while, then concluded his report with, 'The only other remark von Islemann was reported to have made about the Reichsführer's recent visit was to the effect that the best silver should be used.' He had made it a boring, neutral report, hard to get a handle on either way. It would bring him neither praise nor blame, and would probably mean that he was left where he was.

*   *   *

148

Later that afternoon the Kaiser and the Princess came as near as was possible, in the Kaiser's eyes, to having a row. It was not conceivable for him to have what he would consider a proper row, a real man's row, with anyone less than a fellow sovereign. Cousin Georgie in England would have been suitable, given what he had done – or not done – to save Tsar Nicholas. A fine, thumping row he would have given Georgie, perhaps even an actual, well-deserved thump, but death had claimed that pleasure first. Well, perhaps they would meet beyond the undiscovered bourn and have it out there, with poor Nicholas himself to referee them. It wouldn't be long now.

Wearying of his chopping, he had come back in for his afternoon nap a little later than usual. Afterwards, when he had just awoken and was beginning to stir – waking and the ability to move no longer coincided as they used to, especially with these confounded pains in his legs – she sailed into his study, arriving in full flow, her long dress billowing behind her, in mid-sentence as though they were already talking. Her hands, her big horny hands, were clasped before her. If she had had the remotest idea how he loved beautiful hands she might have had the decency to hide her own. He hated being walked in on before he was ready to deal with the world.

'So it is clear I must go to Berlin and follow up on the good relationship we have begun,' were the first words he heard, before he could turn his head. 'And I must secure an introduction to Herr Hitler in order to negotiate his introduction to you so that you can make suitable arrangements for your return to the throne. But I should not mention that yet, do you think, my darling?' She stood smiling down at him and rubbing her great hands.

'To Berlin? You? Now?' He struggled to his feet, his

calves suddenly aching as if he had walked from St Petersburg. He was momentarily breathless. 'To see that man Himmler again?'

'On your behalf, my darling.'

The Kaiser felt he might explode. His right hand shook. This was worse than Bismarck. 'And what if I do not wish it? If I wish never to talk to these people again? If I wish that no one – no one on God's earth, no matter who they are or think they are – should talk to these people on my behalf? What if that is my wish, eh?'

Her face went very quickly from determined smile to wide-eyed indignation, as if she might have been prepared for this. 'Willie, you cannot afford these attitudes. You cannot be like this any longer. Such self-indulgence is ridiculous nowadays. What does it matter if the Nazis are not nobility? They are the people in power, the people we have to deal with. For you to refuse Herr Hitler an audience, under the right circumstances, is an abdication of responsibility.'

Later, he admitted to himself it was the word 'abdication' that had done it. He could not abide that word used in relation to himself and he yielded to anger in a way he had not done for years. Yet even as he permitted it to lift and carry him like a great surging wave he was aware that he could have chosen not to, that he could have stepped aside from it. This was his real self-indulgence, not what she thought. He shouted and ranted, his eyebrows rising and falling with his voice, his cheeks quivering and his good arm gesticulating, though he felt like doing so much more with it. These Nazis were terrible people, he stormed at her, worse than animals. The visit had been a success from only one point of view – Himmler's – and that was all that mattered so far as he was concerned. In every other way it had been a disaster, a scandalous occasion. She was worse than stupid if she could not see that. He wanted absolutely nothing more to do with the Nazis than he absolutely had to, and he absolutely forbade her to go to Berlin and talk to them on his behalf. It was mad, undignified, humiliating to crawl to them. Worse, it would be a public and international scandal. These were not people one should have anything to do with. That was nothing to do with their birth but everything to do with the gangsters they were. Did she not see that? Was she a moose or an elk not to see what was before her eyes, to understand what that hollow man, that husk of a fellow, was saying?

Krebbs, returning to his desk in the corridor, heard her protestations from the top of the stairs.

'Willie – it is our good fortune – your good fortune – that Herr Himmler approves of us!' she exclaimed, almost breathless with indignation, injury and her sense of injustice. 'If he did not we would be paupers begging on the streets of Berlin or working our hands to the bone in prison. It is because you know this in your heart that you cannot forgive him and his party anything they do. It is pride in you, you hate to acknowledge your own dependence. But you are dependent and thanks to the support of the Nazi leadership – and some thanks to your wife, too – you are highly regarded. Do you not see that?'

The Kaiser replied as if through clenched teeth. 'So, Hermine, you would have me dance like a puppet before these people, on strings, to dignify their show. You would have the Kaiser jerk and twitch and grin whenever Heinrich Himmler, the schoolmaster's son, snaps his fingers. That is what you are asking me to do, don't you see? And I become part of the show to distract attention from their disgusting fouling of their own nest, which is also Germany's nest, our nest. That is what you want, is it, my darling?'

The sarcasm of his last words made her pause. When she replied her tone was one of wounded dignity, restrained and hurt. 'It may not have been apparent to you, Willie, but Herr Himmler impressed me and everyone else who took the trouble to listen to him as a natural gentleman. He was polite and considerate and generous. He is easily our best hope. We must be logical.'

There was a longer pause, after which the Kaiser spoke reflectively, as if considering an archaeological exhibit. 'That man is from another planet. He is not like us. He is not of us. There is something missing in him. He is a man without – without – that is what he is, a man without. And he is low. I do not mean low-born, but low in his behaviour. Little things matter more to him than big things, which he does not see. Method, process, details, rules are his angels, and that jumped-up corporal, that failed Viennese artist, his god. He and all his kind, they are the sort who would take money from you.'

The Princess uttered a guttural noise, a mixture of snort and cry. 'I don't care! I don't care what you say! I am going to Berlin!'

She swept out of the room and past Krebbs, her eyes glassy with emotion, her heavy features baffled and determined. He felt the warm wind of her dress.

The ripples of the row surged through the household. When, shortly afterwards, Krebbs went down to the kitchen, the cooks already knew of it. In the hall two whispering maids fell silent when he passed. The Princess's personal maid was summoned to help her pack, the railway timetable was called for, a car and driver were summoned. When Krebbs returned to his desk with the coffee he had ordered from the kitchen, there was no sound from the Kaiser's study, only the smell of a newly-lit cigar. He peered through the crack in the door but could see nothing. The gatehouse rang to say that a despatch rider had arrived with

152

another signal. He sealed and addressed his report on von Islemann so that the man could take it back with him.

'Untersturmführer, are you there?'

'Yes, your Highness.'

The Kaiser was seated on his saddle chair in his inner sanctum. He appeared to be writing, his cigar smouldering in the ashtray beside him. 'Tell me why you joined the Waffen SS,' he said, without looking round.

Krebbs was surprised. No one had asked since his initial interview when they had confirmed that he was over five feet ten and checked his health and fitness. 'I wished to be at the heart of things,' he said, 'to be involved. I had heard they were an elite and I wanted to be part of the new Germany. I wanted to serve where I could serve best and be most demanded of.'

'And they have not disappointed you?'

'No, sire.' He was still addressing the Kaiser's rear.

The old man's head nodded slowly. 'I might have done the same in your position.'

Krebbs thought of the withered arm, the self-awarded medals, the three hundred dress uniforms, the mottled and whiskered old ears that had never heard a shot fired in anger, but didn't smile. The old man's illusions now seemed to him more sad than funny or distasteful. And, although it was impossible to imagine the Kaiser as a young man, he might have tried to join, he really might.

The Kaiser turned in his saddle with obvious effort. His face was blotched. 'You find that hard to believe, of course.' He smiled lugubriously at Krebbs's hesitation. 'Your silence does you credit. Now tell me, as part of the new elite, do you really believe that Germany can win this war?'

'Yes, so long as we believe in ourselves and organise ourselves properly.'

'And do not fight on two fronts and do not take on

the whole world and do not allow ourselves to be led by men from other planets.' The Kaiser spoke with sudden passion, staring at Krebbs as if the choices were all his. 'I do not mean our modern generals who are better than my own were, I mean our leadership, your leadership. Do you not see that these men are incomplete? They are shells with undeveloped souls rattling around inside. They will betray anything and everything because they believe only in themselves but know not themselves, know not what shells they are. They are madmen. And that is why they do not know what other people are, which is why they can do terrible things and not see why it matters. And so they cannot see how completely they, in turn, will be destroyed, our nation with them.' The Kaiser continued staring, his eyes wide, breathing as if from exertion. 'They are men of dreams,' he said, more calmly, 'who lead us sleepwalking into their own nightmare.'

Krebbs said nothing.

'I do not expect you to answer,' the Kaiser continued. 'For you, even to whisper such thoughts into your pillow is to undermine the faith required of you. There is no scope in the life you have chosen for question, argument or reservation. There is nothing between loyalty absolute, loyalty to every jot and tittle of the creed, and treason. You long to give loyalty and commitment. I understand that. It was the same for me. It still is. But your cause is not one that is strengthened by questioning, Untersturmführer. It is dangerous for you even to listen to an old man's rambling. They would call it treachery. Has the Princess departed yet?'

'She is packing. A car has been summoned.'

The Kaiser turned back to his desk. 'Order me coffee, if you would be so kind.'

The despatch rider's signal, marked urgent, was from HQ SS. It reported a further clandestine transmission, giving

154

date and time. The secret monitoring unit was confident that the transmitter could be precisely located if monitoring could be conducted from within the Doorn estate. The unit was therefore on its way to Doorn where Krebbs was required to accommodate it secretly in the gatehouse, since that was entirely under Wehrmacht control and only military personnel permitted. They would arrive that evening. No one in the household was to know. In order to explain any extra vehicles or personnel Krebbs was to say that his SS superior, Colonel Kaltzbrunner, was coming to inspect Krebbs and his men, and to review arrangements for the Kaiser's security. Colonel Kaltzbrunner would be accommodated within the house and would indeed conduct an inspection of the household.

Krebbs read the signal twice, experiencing for the first time the physical meaning of the phrase, heavy-hearted. It was as if a weight grew within him, holding him down, spreading lethargy and reluctance, robbing him of energy and purpose. It took an effort of will to lift the telephone receiver but once he was talking to the gatehouse the need to keep up appearances galvanised him. He explained the requirement, ordered dispositions and cancelled, for the second time, home leave for those who were due it. Then, locking the signal in his security box, he straightened his uniform, put on his cap and strode to the stairs, mounting them three at a time. On the way, through one of the windows, he saw the Princess getting into the car, but he did not pause. From the top of the stairs he crossed to the servants' staircase, pausing at the bottom to listen before ascending carefully, on the balls of his feet.

Again, she was not there, which was as he expected. Except that the bed was made and her clothes tidied away, it was as he had left it early that morning. He leant his back against the door for a few seconds, indulging himself in the sense of her presence. He could hear her voice, things she had said or that he imagined her saying, more clearly than he could picture her face. That was curious, because he had always thought of his memory as photographic. It was her eyes he recalled most clearly, grey, quiet, but playful. The narrow bed looked trim and celibate now.

He crossed the room to the eaves cupboard and pulled out her two brown suitcases, lifting the smaller one on to the bed. It was heavier than the other and locked by two catches. He searched all the obvious places for the key and felt inside the cupboard. He needed a screwdriver really but his pocket-knife would have to do, if it were strong enough. He forced the blade beneath the catch and pulled, at the same time pushing the front of the lock. First one catch, then, with more of a struggle, the other, sprang open.

Inside was a matt black Morse receiver and transmitter with black buttons, brass switches, a single large dial and a disconnected battery packed tightly in at the side. No wonder she had lowered it so carefully to the floor when finding him there the day before. 'Hiding in the woods and signalling to the enemy,' had been her disarmingly direct answer to his direct question. Presumably, going to bed with him was a further disarming mechanism designed to prevent or neuter further questions. His sharp resentment at being used in this way came gilded with the pleasure of righteousness. He was still on his knees, fingering the cold little switches and nourishing his resentment, when she appeared in the doorway.

'So, you have betrayed the Fatherland,' he said.

She pushed the door to and leaned against it as he had, her hands behind her. She was looking at the transmitter rather than him. 'You have to belong in order to betray.'

'You have betrayed me.'

'I told you what I was doing.'

'You made it sound like a joke.'

'You heard what you wanted to hear.'

156

He stood. 'Now I must arrest you and hand you over to security for interrogation. They have been monitoring your transmissions. They are cleverer than you think. They know the transmissions are coming from this house or this park. The next time, the next time you did it, they would have caught you.'

She nodded indifferently, as if they were discussing someone else. 'I have transmitted too often, stayed too long, tried too hard.'

'What at? What are you doing?'

'I told you what I've been doing, when you asked me, last night.'

'You said you were here to find out what the Kaiser wants. Wants in respect of what? Who sent you? Where are you from? And what were you going to do when you found out what he wants?'

She glanced at the party wall, indicating that he was becoming too loud, went to the bed and sat on it. Gently, she closed the suitcase, crossed her legs and clasped her hands around her knee. 'If you really want to discuss all this, you might at least sit down and take off your cap.'

He hesitated. To acquiesce would seem a concession, but to remain standing virtually at attention was absurd. He had always felt that somehow she directed him and until now hadn't minded, so long as he also felt she liked him. It was actually quite nice, as he had put it to himself. But now her manner was as if she were dealing with a recalcitrant child. He resisted for a while longer, then took off his cap and sat. He caught the ghost of a smile in her eyes, and had to stop himself returning it.

'My name really is Akki,' she said, 'I really do come from Friesland, I really am Jewish, as I told you. I have never told you an untruth, I have simply not told you the full truth. The rest is that my parents left Holland for England, with me, long before this war. I finished my schooling in England and became a teacher. When the war started in 1939 – for England – Holland was not, of course, involved, at least not directly, until the Germans invaded. Nevertheless, I volunteered for war work in England and after a while I was selected, because of my languages, for what they called "liaison duties" and soon I found I was working for the British secret service. They asked me – they did not order or send me – if I would return to Holland to make contact with the Kaiser in order to see whether he were prepared to defect to England as a protest at what the Nazis were doing, and perhaps to act as a figurehead for German resistance to Hitler. If he were willing, I was to arrange for his exfiltration. If he were not, well and good, I have to arrange for my own. There was no plan to kidnap or kill him or anything like that. They had been ordered, they told me, by Mr Churchill to discover the Kaiser's views as urgently as possible. That is why I am here, Martin. There is nothing else.'

At first he could think of nothing to say; it was so extraordinary, and so credible, so apparently everyday, and as undoubtedly dangerous. There seemed no appropriate response, but he was determined to say something. 'Are you the age you told me when I was completing the form on you?'

She laughed. It was as if they were having dinner together, relaxing and drinking. 'Are you worried the form might be misleading? That is so typical of your people. Inaccuracy would never do, would it? Martin, I am the age I told you. Why should I lie about it? It's true that I am older than you and I am a little embarrassed about it, but not too seriously. Unless it matters to you?'

Krebbs did not laugh. 'Why did you get involved with me?'

'That was my first mistake.' She watched the effect of her words. 'I don't mean because I do not like you. I do, very

much. Perhaps you find that hard to believe. I think you
are not very used to close relations with women. I don't
mean just going to bed, I mean being intimate, sharing
yourself. Also, you were dangerous because you are SS
and because of your task here. It was safer to get to know
you and follow what you were doing. Then, when you
seemed to want to get to know me very well, it was better
not to make an enemy of you by refusing.'

'So you did it in order to find out things?'

'Only partly.'

'You went to bed with me last night to stop me finding
out what you had been doing?'

'Only partly, as I said. After all, I told you the truth when
you asked. You know that now. I could easily have lied.'
There was silence. 'Does it upset you?'

'No, of course not. I just want to know before I turn
you in, that's all.' He spoke roughly.

'It does, doesn't it? You are upset. I was right about you.
You are nicer than you think you are, perhaps nicer than
you want to be, though probably you don't like my saying
so. I promise you, Martin, I would not have permitted you
in my bed if I did not like you.'

'What does the Kaiser know about this?'

She looked at her knee and shin, as if inspecting a stock-
ing for ladders. 'He knows of the offer and has not accepted
it. He has not rejected it, but I think non-acceptance must
constitute rejection.'

'Why are you still here, then?'

'That was my second mistake. I should have gone. I
was supposed to leave as soon as I had any indication
of his position, and I realised early on, even before I
had a chance to speak to him, but I stayed for Herr
Himmler's visit. Not only to observe Himmler and perhaps to learn something of what is planned, but to see
whether it would have any effect on the Kaiser, whether

it would make him change his mind, or even go back to Germany.'

'And?'

'I think he was shocked by what Himmler said about the Jewish children, don't you?'

Krebbs was finding it hard to maintain his anger. He wanted to feel it, and to show it – to shout it – but conversation with her absorbed it like seawater in sand. 'It has had an effect. But he says hard things about the Jews himself.'

'And you, were you not shocked, Martin?' There was a sudden fullness in her eyes that he had not seen before. It thrilled him to be the focus of such attention, even in these circumstances. 'Paradis was bad enough, this is something worse. Far, far worse. A different league of thing altogether.'

'Spies are executed. They would call what you are doing spying. You would be shot.'

'Martin, answer me.' Her knuckles, clasped across her knee, were white with pressure.

He sat still, cap in lap, as for a photograph, but felt as though he were wriggling. 'Yes, it is wrong. But it is not –'

'No buts.' She leaned forward, her eyes like hard grey stones.

He changed position. 'He knows who sent you, the Kaiser? Which means that the Kaiser talks to the Reichsführer about returning to Berlin while at the same time he is in treasonable communication with the enemy?'

'Martin,' she said again.

Krebbs thought of his mother and sister, of what they would think. 'Yes, it is wrong. Very wrong. It is terrible to kill children.'

'Even if they are Jewish?'

'Yes.'

She relaxed. 'He will never return to Berlin now. He will die at Doorn, I am sure.'

'So von Islemann says.' He paused. 'Does von Islemann know about this English offer?'

'Possibly. His Highness is open with him.'

'And, if so, does he know about you?'

'Possibly.'

'Or even us – you and I?'

'One never knows what people notice.'

Her manner was nonchalant now, her tone subdued. He suspected it might be a pose. 'Aren't you worried by this? Aren't you frightened? You should be. The more people who know, the more likely someone will report. And why did the English send you, knowing you were Jewish? It's more dangerous for Jews. Or didn't you tell them?'

'There is no point in worrying about what is beyond my control. I volunteered for this. It is not my profession but it was something I could do, and I wanted to do something. As for my being Jewish, of course they know. You don't have to hide it there. And it's because I'm Jewish that I came. I thought you would understand that. Now I must go.' Her eyes no longer met his but seemed focused on her knee. 'Of course I would be frightened, if I let myself, but the time for fear is before and after something, not while you are doing it.'

He realised that for some time he had been sitting just as she was, legs crossed, the polished toe of his boot before him. She must have noticed it, too. It was becoming ridiculous. He stood, in a last effort to assert himself. 'You appreciate that I have power of life and death over you? And that the Gestapo would do terrible things to you? They would make you confess your escape route, the people who would help you, times, addresses, everything?' He pictured her strapped across a torture table, naked, quivering, bloodied, screaming, but

161

stopped himself. Even to picture it was somehow to will it. 'It is my duty to hand you over. I have the power to do it.'

She looked up again. 'Martin, you have absolute power over me except for one thing: you could not have made me like you against my will. That was my third mistake.'

'It doesn't matter whether you like me or not. You did it for your own reasons.'

She shrugged and leaned back on the bed, propped on one elbow. 'If I didn't like you, would it matter to me what you think? Would I risk myself by being honest with you? And would I still want you?'

When he awoke the rain was beating against the dormer window and the wind whistling through the woodwork, rattling the panes. The rain had made dusk come early. His boots were on their sides on the floor, his uniform scattered. Her dress was crumpled between the bed and the wall. The small brown suitcase squatted balefully on the floor.

Her head pressed heavily on his arm, her hair splayed across the pillow and her cheek, her lips parted in sleep. He could not see his watch without disturbing her and so tried carefully to lift and turn his head, to see her clock. From outside, at intervals through the rain, came a distant, occasional knock. She would be missed at her duties now, surely, whatever they were. And he at his. Please God, he thought, that Colonel Kaltzbrunner and his team have not arrived. Kaltzbrunner was a mean man, coarse, cruel, hatchet-hard, built like a bull, a drunkard, a bully and a lawyer, an Austrian lawyer at that. Krebbs wanted to stay as he was, where he was, for ever, postponing everything, but the image of Kaltzbrunner poisoned all. It was to Kaltzbrunner that he should hand her over.

'It can't be him, surely.' She lifted her head suddenly, just above him, her hair brushing his face.

'What? Who?' He was still thinking of Kaltzbrunner.

She listened, her mouth half open. There was another distant knock. 'It is him, it's the Kaiser chopping wood.' She pulled at his watch on his recumbent arm. 'At this time of day and in this rain, he must be mad or unwell.'

'He likes to chop wood. He often does it. You know that.'

'Not in the rain, he hates rain. He must be ill or unhappy.'

'He can't be ill if he's chopping wood.'

She climbed over him and went to the window where she stood listening, her back to him. The rain greeted her with another fusillade. He began to want her again. She turned. 'We must go and see if he's all right.'

'What? Why?' He laughed. She looked ridiculously concerned.

'I'm sure he isn't well. I'll go.' She began picking up her clothes.

'You like the old man, don't you? You have a soft spot for him.'

'He has a soul.'

Krebbs sprang out of bed. 'You can't go out in this. It will look suspicious to the guards. Everyone will ask questions. I'll go.'

Luckily, he met no one on the stairs and a call to the gatehouse confirmed that the monitoring team had not arrived. He was late for his own inspection but told them there would be none that evening. Downstairs he met two of the staff who explained with worried haste and wringing hands that the Kaiser was out chopping wood in the rainstorm, when it was almost time for his dinner. He was a man of such regular routine where meals were concerned that everyone was perplexed. No one had been out to see him, however; without von Islemann or the Princess, they weren't sure what to do. Krebbs said he would go and fetch him in.

He took his torch from his kitbag, put on his cape and pulled his cap firmly on before opening the front door and filling the hall and stairs with a great wet gust. He made a cursory inspection of his dripping sentries first, confirming that they had not seen the Kaiser return, then headed across the sodden lawns towards the woodshed in the trees. It was lighter out than it had appeared from within and he did not yet need the torch. The wind tossed the tree-tops, flattened the longer grass in capricious waves, sent the bottom of his cape flapping against his legs one moment and tugging away the next. It was worse than the night before. In the pauses between gusts he listened vainly for the fall of the axe until, as he was entering the trees, he heard it once, sharply and distinctly. For a moment he wondered whether it was really the Kaiser after all, or whether there might have been some fantastic happening and he would find an enraged Dutchman chopping the Kaiser. He checked his pistol in its holster.

The woodshed was screened by trees and faced away from the house, so he had to walk round it to see anything. He trod softly, though even in the lulls there was enough noise from the wind and dripping branches to mask his footsteps. The Kaiser was outside the shed, his axe on the chopping block propping him up as he leant on it, breathing heavily and irregularly, occasionally gasping. He was hatless and in his field grey uniform, his tunic unbuttoned, showing his braces and crumpled, soaking shirt. The wind played with his grey hair, unheeded. Even in the gloom, his face looked unusually pale. The dog, Wei-wei, sheltered beneath the woodshed roof and for once did not yelp at Krebbs, gazing with morose indifference. Arno was nowhere to be seen. The Kaiser, too, watched Krebs approach, his gaze glacial and strange.

'You,' he said, between laboured breaths. 'I thought the other, the girl, might come. Hermine is in Berlin.'

Krebs had to stand close to be heard. 'Are you well, your Highness? Your face is pale. It is late to be out.'

'I am better than you will ever be, Untersturmführer, if you stay in. Better get out while you can.' He stooped and, with his withered left arm, nudged the split log on the block so that it was broadside on to him. Then he heaved the axe back with his right arm and, with a twist of his entire upper body, grunted and swung it down. It was a perfect cut, the two quarters toppling off the block to join the spreading pile beneath. He leant again upon his axe and turned to Krebs. 'Bismarck could not have done that if he had lived to be a hundred and eighty.'

'This rain is bad for you, your Highness, and it is past suppertime.'

'I am past my own time, young man. I have seen enough. I have pains in my chest, in my legs and under my arms.' He paused, breathing heavily, then seemed to gather energy and spoke loudly and rapidly. 'My joints are out of time, the times are out of joint as your Shakespeare – her Shakespeare, his, Churchill's Shakespeare – would have said. Did say. Those words will do, they will serve. You know Shakespeare?'

'I know of him.'

'Wodehouse knows him. So does the boy Churchill. You will hear a lot from him before this war is over. It's all he knows. Help me, would you.'

He spoke the last words calmly as his axe fell to the ground, his head drooped and he began to subside on to the chopping block. Krebs's arms were slightly constricted by his cape but he stepped forward and grabbed the old man, trying to ease him into a sitting position on the block. The weight was unwieldy, causing him to slip and stumble among the wet logs, forcing him to his knees. He was not trained to deal with heart attacks, if that was what was happening; there were no elderly men in the Waffen SS. He said what he thought afterwards were stupid, unnecessary, superfluous things – where did it hurt, could he breathe, not to worry because he would telephone for a doctor and there was the hospital the Kaiser himself had had built in the next village, could he sit upright while Krebbs ran for help, was he warm enough, did he want Krebbs's cape, wouldn't he prefer to lie down. His cap came off in the struggle, the rain beat hard on his bare head, running down his neck inside his collar and up his sleeves as he tried to keep the Kaiser from toppling on to the logs surrounding the block. He slithered and scrambled as they cut into his knees and soaked his trousers. For periods the Kaiser appeared not to be breathing at all, then would fetch one long, shuddering breath, guttural and animal. The rain made a continuous, drenching noise through the trees, drowning out everything else.

'Better you lie down!' Krebbs shouted in his ear. 'I'll kick away some logs and make a space.'

He tried but they were too many and too slippery for him to get any purchase while he fought to support the old man, whose heavy upper body threatened constantly to fall in any direction. Once, after a long time without a breath, the Kaiser's wet head lolled against Krebbs's face, resting heavily against his cheek, and Krebbs wondered if he were already dead. But then there was another great juddering breath and he spoke again.

'Tell the Princess.'

'Yes, I will, don't worry, it's all right, I will.' He was breathless himself now and sweating inside his uniform.

He did not notice Akki until the Kaiser himself raised his right arm at her hooded figure. She had her coat over her head, holding it together across her throat.

Rain dripped from the Kaiser's uplifted nose and chin, coursing down his cheeks. 'Mama,' he said. 'Such hands.' He struggled to raise his right arm, his good arm. 'Yours like hers.' She came closer, stumbling on the logs, and took his hand in her own. 'Hands,' he whispered again, then suddenly, in his normal voice and with theatrical gallantry, he said, *'Dürfte ich ihre Hand küssen?'* She nodded and knelt by him. His head bent over her hand and he pressed it to his lips. He clung to it as his body again began tilting away from Krebbs, who scrambled and slipped to hold him.

'Lay him down, he needs space to lie but I can't move the logs without letting go,' panted Krebbs.

The Kaiser shuddered and lifted his head. Akki's hand was still in his, forcing her to let go of her coat and practically sprawl across the logs. His flesh darkened and his eyes were strangely flat. 'Thank Churchill,' he said. 'Tell him I stay. I run no more. Look to yourselves.'

Krebbs's face and the Kaiser's were almost touching. 'Don't try to speak, don't worry,' he said. 'We'll lie you down, we'll clear a space.'

Akki freed herself and began clearing the split logs. As she made room Krebbs allowed the Kaiser to tip the way his heavy body wanted to go, easing him down carefully. They laid him on his side, his head resting on his right arm. Krebbs looked at her. Her hair had come loose and was plastered against her face. She was panting. 'Run back to the sentries by the house,' he said. 'Get them to telephone the gatehouse from the phone outside my room and send four men up with one of the folding camp beds. Tell the gatehouse to telephone for a doctor. We'll carry him into the house.'

167

She was looking down at the Kaiser's head, which had slipped off his arm and was resting on the earth, as if he were kissing it. Krebbs lifted it with both hands while she pushed the arm back under. It was a dead weight. She stroked the Kaiser's hair back. 'I don't think we need hurry.'

For a while it seemed that the world was the rain, spattering on the logs around them and sounding in the leaves above like static on direction-finding radios, only less harsh. It fell like pellets on the back of his head where his hair was short.

'You must go. Now,' he said eventually. 'They – Himmler's people – suspect something. They are surrounding the park. If you don't go now you will be arrested and I will not be able to help you.'

'And shot. I know.' She spoke quietly, her face still lowered so that rain dripped from her on to the Kaiser's matted grey hair.

'Shot if you're lucky.'

'I was fond of him. Weren't you?' Her wet face turned to his.

Krebbs stood. Were you as fond of me? he almost asked. And send no signals, he almost added, but conscience stopped him. There was no need to let the enemy know everything about the monitoring. 'Just go.'

She stood. 'Goodbye, Martin.'

He mumbled something but wasn't himself sure what. It was lost, anyway, in his hurried, fumbling grabbing and kissing her. He pulled her to him so hard that her teeth knocked against his, trapping his lip. He tasted blood in his mouth. Somewhere in the park a lorry revved its engine several times. He pushed her away. 'Go.'

Krebbs went to Huis Doorn to break the news, instructing that von Islemann be contacted and ordered back from leave. He would know how to contact the Princess. Then he went to the gatehouse himself. The monitoring team, he had been warned, had arrived. As he approached he made out the tall figure of Colonel Kaltzbrunner who stood, legs apart, arms behind his back, before a couple of lorries. Another lorry, the familiar Wehrmacht ration lorry, was just pulling in behind them. The colonel returned Krebbs's 'Heil Hitler!' salute with aggressive precision but no hint of recognition, though they had met several times.

'I have to report the death of the Kaiser, sir. He has just died.'

'How?'

'Of natural causes. Probably his heart.'

'One less burden on the state. It need not affect our work here. Come inside.'

The gatehouse was busy, with both Wehrmacht and SS staff personnel. Krebbs's soldiers went about their duties with serious expressions. Equipment had already been unloaded from the two lorries and installed in one of the upper rooms. The atmosphere was tense.

'If he so much as squeaks at any time from now on, we shall have him,' said Kaltzbrunner, grinning as they went upstairs. 'We are listening already.'

The room was blacked out and the lighting subdued. Uniformed operators wearing headphones sat at two bulky receivers with large dials and fine tuning needles, which the operators revolved continuously by turning fat knobs. Whooshes and squeaks came through the ether, each abruptly cut off as the needle moved on.

'Yes,' said Kaltzbrunner, nodding, 'if he speaks again tonight we shall silence him for good. Now, Krebbs, you have arranged accommodation and dinner for me in the house? I am looking forward to seeing this house, especially now that I do not have to make polite conversation with its owner.' He laughed.

Krebbs knew there would be something ready because the cook had already prepared the Kaiser's. 'I think we may be eating his dinner, sir.'

'And toasting our success with his wine, I hope.'

The rain had lessened now and they walked together up the drive in the dark, precisely in step. Kaltzbrunner was in good humour. 'I have read your reports and of course I was briefed on the Reichsführer's visit. It is tempting to arrest the suspect von Islemann immediately but if, as is possible, he is also responsible for these transmissions, then it is better to leave him and catch him in the act. Where is he at this moment?'

'He was at his house in the village. He has been informed of the Kaiser's death and will come up to the house to begin arrangements. He should be here soon.' Krebbs paused. 'But I don't think he can be guilty of anything, sir. I don't think he is sending these signals.'

'Why not?'

'I was with him during the times given for one of the transmissions.' It was worse than a lie; it was spontaneous, with no prepared back-up. He owed no loyalty to von Islemann beyond the simple statement of his opinion, surely; but he didn't regret it. He felt decisive and confident, as if something problematic had at last been resolved.

'He may have an accomplice. I went through the list of staff you sent. All have been here a long time except one of the maids. The transmissions began only after her arrival. We should have her in for investigation, too.'

Their boots crunched in perfect co-ordination on the gravel. It was a comforting sound.

'I have looked into von Islemann's background,' continued Kaltzbrunner. 'He is typical of the old military class that seeks to frustrate everything the Führer is trying to do for Germany and for Aryan peoples everywhere. At the very least we must satisfy ourselves that his attitudes have been reformed and are correct. Your report was unclear on that aspect. We must find out. What is your opinion?'

'So far as I could tell, sir, he is patriotic and does nothing to oppose the new Reich.'

'But he does not love us.'

The house was in a state of quiet confusion. Everyone felt the need to be present but no one knew what to do. They talked about what had happened and sought comfort in repeating themselves. Everything was waiting for von Islemann; he would know how to contact the Princess, would make decisions about the body, would know how to proceed.

Krebbs had no difficulty getting dinner served in the small dining-room after he had shown Kaltzbrunner to the rooms occupied by the Reichsführer. The staff were relieved to have that to do, and were gratified that the fish prepared for the Kaiser was not to be wasted.

They were eating when von Islemann arrived. Hearing him in the hall, Krebbs went through and drew him aside from the others. 'Colonel Kaltzbrunner is here looking for spies. He wishes to meet you.'

Von Islemann raised his fine eyebrows. 'Does he imagine I can help him?'

'They are suspicious of your attitude because of the questions you asked the Reichsführer. They are also looking for more serious things and are ready to arrest anyone. They are certain there is a spy here.'

'Hence the new arrivals at the gatehouse with their special aerials?'

'No one is supposed to know that.'

'Then they should tell them not to call out instructions to each other.'

Krebbs was impatient; they had only a few seconds. 'You

don't understand. It is dangerous here now for everyone. If they do not catch a real spy they will be determined to find a substitute. You would do very nicely for them. Be careful.'

'But there never was a real spy, was there? No one was actually spying on anyone. And now, with His Highness dead, everything will change, no more questions, no answers needed, certain people will move on. I hope you will permit that, though it may be sad for you.'

He continued before Krebbs could react. 'Now you must introduce me. I shall be brief. And in case there is not another chance, Martin, I should like to say how pleased I am that you have become, after all, more one of us than one of them. Good luck in your war.'

He turned and opened the door to the dining-room, advancing confidently upon Kaltzbrunner and taking his hand before he was fully out of his seat. 'A sad occasion for your first visit to Huis Doorn, Herr Colonel, and particularly sad for you not to have met His late Majesty in person.'

Kaltzbrunner grinned, showing some potato in his mouth. 'So be it. We have little time for history now that we are busy making it and anyway we are benefiting, as you see, from Prince Wilhelm's loss of appetite.'

'Indeed, a sensible precaution against hungry times ahead. His Majesty would doubtless have approved. And now, if you will forgive me, Herr Colonel, I must make arrangements for the body.'

'Heil Hitler!' Kaltzbrunner saluted challengingly as von Islemann turned away. Krebbs automatically followed suit.

Von Islemann merely nodded his acknowledgement, then turned to Krebbs. 'Herr Untersturmführer, may I request the use of your ration lorry which I noticed at the gatehouse to take the remains to the morgue?'

'Ask the duty corporal outside to ring the gatehouse and tell them to send it up,' said Krebbs.

'There, you see,' said Kaltzbrunner as they sat again after the door had closed. 'People give themselves away in such matters. Is he Jewish? He looks as if he could be.'

'I don't believe so, sir.'

'You never know, it is not always easy to tell. Have you checked whether any of the staff are Jewish?'

'Yes, sir.'

'And are they?'

'No, sir.'

They took their coffees upstairs afterwards because Kaltzbrunner wanted to see the Kaiser's study. While they were there the gatehouse rang for him on Krebbs's phone. Krebbs handed him the receiver and watched his face stiffen. He gave orders for the house to be surrounded and for an NCO and snatch squad to meet him at the front door immediately. His expression, when he put down the phone, was one of triumphant resolve. 'We have him,' he whispered. 'He is on air now, from this very house. We shall secure it and search it from top to bottom. First, where is von Islemann?'

'We left him downstairs, sir.'

Kaltzbrunner ran down without waiting for Krebbs who, as soon as his colonel was out of sight, ran up the stairs. Surely she had gone. She must have. He paused at the bottom of the servants' stairs, then went quietly. Her door was shut. At first there was resistance, as if someone were pushing against him, but when he shoved hard it yielded, sliding her big suitcase along the floor. The other was on the bed, open. She was kneeling before it, still in her wet clothes, and wearing headphones, her finger on the Morse key, her novel and a ruler beside it.

He felt like shouting, but spoke calmly. 'They're coming.

They're monitoring your transmission. They know you're here. Stop it now.' He took his pistol from his holster and cocked it.

She took off her headphones and stood. For the first time since he had known her she looked frightened. 'I had to, I had to signal to initiate my exfiltration. If I can get to the coast –' She spoke stiffly, then stopped, looking from his pistol to his face.

He eased the safety catch off with a discreet click. If he were to do it, it should be now. There would never be another chance. He could say she had attacked him, tried to jump out of the window, anything. She was looking into his eyes, her lips parted, her own eyes unusually wide. She had re-tied her wet hair since the woods but a strand had come loose. He pointed the pistol just below her left breast. It wouldn't stay still.

'Are you going to?' she asked. Her voice faltered, almost to a whisper. 'Martin, are you really going to do it?'

Carefully, watching the rise and fall of her breast, he took up the first trigger pressure. A fraction more, the slightest contraction of his forefinger, would do it. Her perfect eyebrows, her still wet cheeks, her clear grey eyes had never seemed more alive to him. He made himself imagine them contorted with screaming pain, a quivering animal. It was the only way. They would shoot or hang her at the end of it, anyway. Better she died now, in an instant too brief for her even to know it, with no suffering. Also, under torture, she would tell them he had known, and done nothing. Then it would be him, and then, perhaps, his mother and sister. 'You did it just to make sure I didn't give you away,' he wanted to say to her, 'isn't that true?' She would admit it, then he would shoot her. Yet he could still taste her, the scent of her skin was still on him.

He lowered the pistol through her belly, her crutch and

her thighs. 'Go down the back stairs to my room.' He was surprised by the ordinariness of his voice and the ease with which, despite the trembling in his hand, he re-holstered the pistol. 'Stay there till I come. Go now.'

She bowed her head and walked past him. He went to her transmitter, tucked the headphones back in, closed the lid, took it to the window and heaved it out. He waited to hear it fall, but heard only the wind and rain. He closed the window and looked once more round the room before leaving. He felt utterly calm.

Downstairs the hall was filling with soldiers. A few confused and fearful staff looked on and Kaltzbrunner stood by the open front door shouting orders to someone outside. Von Islemann was by him, pale with anger.

Kaltzbrunner turned to von Islemann. 'I don't care what you say, it is a military lorry under military command. I am ordering it to move this instant.'

Von Islemann spoke with contemptuous deliberation. 'It will move within minutes when the driver returns. He is helping with the body. We have no coffin, as I told you, Herr Colonel, so it has to be wrapped and restrained to prevent it rolling about on the floor of the lorry. If we wait for the undertakers with a coffin it would take longer and word would get out and disaffected elements might abuse it in some way. You worry about disaffected elements, I believe. It is better we take it ourselves to the mortician for preparation, then back here to lie in state. The lorry is not preventing you from searching the house and will very soon be gone. It would have gone already if you had let me out to resume my supervision of arrangements.'

Kaltzbrunner's reply was forestalled by an NCO, to whom he turned for a murmured, urgent conversation. He appeared to forget about von Islemann and, spotting Krebbs, beckoned him urgently. 'Where the hell have you been? Never mind now. He's gone off air but they're almost sure he is somewhere on the top floor, probably in the attic. We're going up now. You know the way. Lead on.'

He drew and cocked his pistol. Krebbs drew his and, watched by the cowed staff, led Kaltzbrunner up the stairs three at a time. They were followed by the NCO and half a dozen soldiers with carbines. This time Krebbs did not pause at the foot of the servants' staircase but crashed up it making plenty of noise. 'The rooms first!' he shouted to Kaltzbrunner. 'The loft entrance is farther along and no one can get out without passing us.'

He barged into the nearest room, which was not hers. The two soldiers with him, without waiting for orders, upturned the bed, yanked the chest of drawers away from the wall, tipping and breaking the vase of flowers on top of it, and crawled into the eaves cupboard. Krebbs could hear the same sort of robust search going on in Akki's room. In each room it was the same. He led the way into the attic, which was huge, dark and dusty, littered with old trunks and lumber. He tried to behave as if he genuinely hoped to find something.

While they were there Kaltzbrunner was summoned from below. Krebbs followed him back down the attic steps. On the landing at the top of the stairs were two of his own sentries, wet and breathless. One held Akki's small brown case, dirty, dented and burst open, the lid hanging now by a single hinge. One of the guards had heard a crash at the back of the house not long ago and had gone to investigate.

Kaltzbrunner took the set, his expression intense, the muscles of his jaw clenched. 'English,' he said to Krebbs. 'We captured an identical one outside Utrecht, with its operator. We'll have this one, too, if he's still in the house. Go downstairs and put all civilians under guard in the hall, including von Islemann. Do a roll-call and see if anyone's missing. Make sure the cordon round the house is tight. No one but military personnel allowed through. We'll search the rest of the loft and then every room downwards, in case he's hiding. Wait for me in the hall.'

Krebbs clattered downstairs but avoided the hall and ran straight down to the kitchen. The cook and two other women who were there talking fell silent and stared. He could tell from the alarm on their faces that his expression was convincing. 'Upstairs! In the hall. Now!' he shouted. For a moment more they stared, open-mouthed. He was still holding his pistol. 'Move!' he shouted. The way they almost fell over each other to get up the stairs would, he thought, have been comical in any other situation. In fact, it was comical if you viewed it in isolation, separating it from everything else. As soon as they were gone he slipped into his own room.

She was sitting on his camp-bed, in her coat. When she stood she left a damp patch on the bed. 'They've found your wireless,' he said. 'No one's allowed out and the house is surrounded. Go up the basement stairs outside this door that leads on to the terrace. At the foot of the house steps is the headquarters ration lorry which is taking the body to the morgue. Walk straight up to it and get into the cab next to the driver. Tell him he's to leave now and that you've been told to accompany the body to the morgue and are to stay there with it. Then he can go back to HQ, which he'll want to do anyway. We don't want him back here talking to anyone. Got that?' She stared. 'D'you understand?'

She nodded, but still said nothing. Krebbs wanted to hit her, shake her and take her at the same time. Even in her fear she was so contained, so unreachable. He wanted to break through to her in some violent, dramatic way, to make her gasp. Instead, he merely spoke. 'You are a bad spy.'

'I know.'

'You realise what I'm doing for you, don't you? You do appreciate it?'

'Yes, Martin, I do.'

'Untersturmführer from now on.' He opened the door and stepped over to her. She stood as if expecting him to embrace her but he put his pistol flat against her back and pushed her roughly through the door. She went up the stone stairs without a backward glance. He waited until her footsteps had faded, then ran up into the hall. The staff were huddled in silent little groups, though there were fewer soldiers than before. Von Islemann stood with his hands clasped behind his back, staring at one of the paintings as if on a leisurely visit to an art gallery. No one was speaking. At the sound of the lorry graunching into first gear and pulling slowly away von Islemann looked round, questioningly.

'Right, pay attention!' Krebbs shouted at the soldiers. 'All staff lined up against that wall and searched.' He gestured at von Islemann with his pistol. 'Including him.'

When the staff were lined up he ordered them all to turn out their pockets, while his soldiers moved along the line body-searching each. Their possessions – handkerchiefs, loose change, pencils, purses, the odd crumpled letter or list – made pathetic little heaps on the floor before them.

Kaltzbrunner reappeared while the search was in progress. 'No one up there. Have you checked the basement?'

'Yes, sir. Nothing found.'

'Anyone missing?'

They were standing near von Islemann, who was at the end of the line. 'One of the maids, the new one.'

'The one I mentioned? The one whose arrival coincided with –?'

'Yes, sir.'

Kaltzbrunner nodded slowly, staring at von Islemann. 'She'll be your spy, then. Question is, was she alone?'

Krebbs was aware of von Islemann staring at him, his eyes filled with accusation, his face livid with contempt. It was impossible to explain. He continued to address Kaltzbrunner. 'She was seen around not long ago, sir, and the cordon's in place, so she won't get far.'

'Let's hope not, Untersturmführer, for your sake.'

'Herr Colonel,' said von Islemann quietly, 'may I be permitted a word on the Untersturmführer's behalf? He is behaving in exemplary fashion, proving beyond my imaginings his loyalty to Shutzstaffel and how good a Nazi he is, after all. I had thought otherwise of him but I see now how foolish I was. I am sure you will both be delighted by the arrest you are about to make. My congratulations to the gallant Untersturmführer.'

Kaltzbrunner's features hardened. He turned to Krebbs. 'I think we'll have him in, don't you? See how he talks then.'

Krebbs did not hesitate. 'If you'll permit me, sir, there's a shorter way with scum like this.' He moved as he spoke, stepping up to von Islemann and murmuring directly at him, 'I got her out. I am doing this for you.' Then, with a wave of his arm like an exaggerated farewell, he swung his pistol against von Islemann's face. It made a heavy, meaty slap and at the same time a curiously muted, hollow sound. Von Islemann made a sound between a gasp and a moan. His legs gave way and he crumpled against the wall, slipping down it to end doubled up on the floor, clutching his face, blood oozing between his slender fingers. No one else moved.

Krebbs holstered his pistol, stepped back and addressed the rest of the staff. 'It was once a serious offence to insult the Kaiser. You all knew that. Now it is the same with all

German officers. This is a lesson everyone must learn.'
He turned to Kaltzbrunner. 'If you agree, sir, I suggest
we leave him to his own lesson, as an example to these
others. He's too stupid and too snobbish to have been in
league with the culprit. He never spoke to servants. If we
concentrate on catching her quickly we'll soon discover if
she had help.'

Kaltzbrunner gazed at von Islemann without expression,
then looked up. 'You're right. Concentrate all forces on
the search. Let this pansy go home and bleed on his own
carpet.'

It was the early hours before the search of the house
and park was called off and the staff allowed to leave the
hall and go to bed. Von Islemann was helped away. The
search would be resumed with first light. Kaltzbrunner
ordered coffee from the exhausted and thoroughly frightened cook. He and Krebbs stood in the kitchen, drinking. 'It's hard to see how she could have got away,'
Kaltzbrunner said. 'Unless she had help locally. We'll
catch her if she hasn't. You can depend on me to do
that. In the morning I want you to question all the staff
again and put down everything that is known about her,
especially details of any friends or acquaintances.'

'Very good, sir.'

'If you can discover anything that leads to her capture, it may still be possible for you to have a career
in security, Krebbs. Otherwise, since an enemy agent
has operated under your very nose throughout the time
the Reichsführer was here, when he might easily have
been assassinated, and then has been allowed to escape,
someone has to take responsibility. It can only be you. You
will return to other duties, to our new war, in the east, to
our imminent Russian front. But maybe you would prefer
that, eh?'

Untersturmführer Krebbs put down his coffee. 'Thank

you, sir. I would prefer that. I wish to get back to real soldiering.'

Kaltzbrunner's grin was comradely. 'Good man. You will find honourable work in Russia, plenty of it. Heil Hitler!'

Untersturmführer Krebbs clicked his heels and saluted.

POSTSCRIPT

This is a fiction, not history or biography. It plays fast and loose with history, not least in its conflation of the years 1940, when the Germans invaded Holland, and 1941, when the Kaiser died and the Germans launched their invasion of Russia. However, some of what is portrayed happened.

Huis Doorn, in which the Kaiser spent most of his exile, survived two invading armies more or less intact; it has in it many of the Kaiser's possessions, including his 'saddle' seat, and is open to the public. He really did fell and plant trees, cultivate his roses, feed his ducks and study archaeology. Some of the more singular remarks he makes in the novel he actually said or wrote. Queen Victoria really did die in his arm.

Churchill offered the Kaiser asylum in Britain (on his – Churchill's – first day in office), though the invitation was not conveyed in the manner shown here. Himmler never visited Huis Doorn, though Goering did (he also accepted money from Princess Hermine). After the German invasion, the Kaiser did indeed have a Wehrmacht guard commanded by an SS officer, although Martin Krebbs is an entirely imagined character. So, too, is Akki. Von Islemann was the name of the Kaiser's real private secretary, who later published a detailed account of the Kaiser's years at Doorn, but the character as portrayed here is, again, entirely imagined. The massacre at Le Paradis, the reprisals following the shooting of SS Gruppenführer Rauter and Himmler's admiration for the most efficient method of murdering Jewish children were all historical.